Death
on the
Home Straight

IRIS V. PENN

Death
on the
Home Straight

IRIS V. PENN

Edited by Chris Newton

MEMOIRS

Cirencester

Published by Memoirs

MEMOIRS
PUBLISHING

Memoirs Books

25 Market Place, Cirencester, Gloucestershire, GL7 2NX
info@memoirsbooks.co.uk www.memoirspublishing.com

ISBN: 9781908223371

Printed in England

CONTENTS

CHAPTER ONE

The word was indelibly printed on my mind – conspiracy. Had Ken just got in the way of the wrong people?

I tried to pull myself together. After all, I reasoned to myself, that sort of thing would never happen in the dignified world of British horse racing.

Again and again I went over the events that had led up to Ken's untimely death, from the morning I had started out so happily to meet him at Kempton. It had been one of those rare, glorious days in October, and on the drive home I remember glancing at the dashboard clock before switching on the radio. I felt the usual ripple of excitement building up inside me as the commentator announced "Racing from Kempton". I knew every first, second and third up to the last race by heart.

I listened intently for the two horses I had backed that afternoon. Good prices they were too – 6-11 and 11-2. I felt my hands beginning to sweat up on the steering wheel.

I knew only too well how temperamental some horses can be before a race, and my pulse was shooting up by the second. It was a toss-up whether I wanted the announcer to get a move on and let us have the result of the 4.30 or prolong the agony and let me live in hope.

This wasn't all due to the fact that I had put ten quid on Music Adored myself, and wanted to make it a hat-trick on the day. Not by a long shot. It was because she was Ken's horse. That was why I so desperately wanted her to win - for his sake.

My fingers were tapping out a tune. "Come on - come on!" I was urging. Every punter knows the feeling.

The radio crackled on. "4.30, Music Adored 11-2..."

Eleven to two! I couldn't believe it. A fantastic price. I would have been more than delighted for it to have been returned at 7-12.

I wondered how Ken was feeling - on cloud nine, I imagined. The only disappointment was that he couldn't be at Catterick to lead her in. He'd had a couple of appointments in town in the morning that he was unable to break, and could only make it to Kempton in time for the second race.

I normally saved all my annual leave to take as single days throughout the season so that I could go to the weekday meetings I liked best - Sandown, Kempton and the other all-round courses where I could follow the horses with my fieldglasses. I can't hear the commentary, you see - bit of a hearing problem and not getting any better.

Newmarket and Doncaster are beautiful courses, but not good for me. On a straight course I can barely pick up the jockeys' hats at the two-furlong marker, and by the time I've sorted them all out it's all over bar the shouting. And the shouting's the only bit I get to hear.

We had a good relationship, Ken and me. We not only shared the same interests - National Hunt Racing, of course, and music - we shared the same office. The place wouldn't have be the same without his unruly mop of dark hair bent over his desk, or the sight of his tall, lean figure striding about. He wasn't exactly handsome, but there was something about his craggy face and kind smile that melted my heart.

What he saw in a five-foot three, slightly overweight, mousey blonde, who was more than a little scatty, always puzzled me. Ken had even asked me to marry him once, being a man of honour, but I had a widow's pension and an interesting job, so I wasn't too keen to give up my independence. And the extra domestic duties that go with marriage didn't appeal to me in the slightest. I put it to him, as gently as possible, that if it was OK by him I was quite happy continuing as we were.

He had seemed quite relieved. He had spent his whole adult life working to achieve his ambition of becoming Underwriter of Livestock at Lloyds, and he'd left it a bit late at fifty to change the scene.

We had left before the last race at Kempton and before the result from Catterick, as Ken had wanted to get back to the office to sign a few letters that had to go out that night. We'd decided to stop off for a meal later. It had become the usual thing for us to splash out on a meal if one of us had had a good winning day. Otherwise we usually picked up some fish and chips at Chris' Plaice, or got a Chinese take-away from Pang's. Not bad, but not up to the standard of the little pub in Essex we had intended to go to, where the food was first-class and the price comparatively reasonable. There we could hold a conversation without having to shout above the music.

I guessed we would be having champagne that evening to celebrate Music Adored's win, as this was something special. I imagine Ken must have been feeling thrilled, particularly as Music Adored was his favourite horse. He loved them all, but none quite so much as Music.

What happened on the drive back will stay in my mind forever.

I remember seeing the rear lights of Ken's BMW two cars ahead of me, just rounding the high curve on the flyover. In my wing-mirror I noticed an HGV coming up in the outside lane. The HGV passed between us and I lost sight of Ken's car for a few seconds. When it eventually appeared again it seemed to be swerving all over the road, as though Ken was drunk, or a tyre had burst. It was completely out of control.

I couldn't imagine what had happened. Perhaps Ken had collapsed - he certainly didn't seem to be making any effort to get the car straightened up. Or had the steering gone?

A few agonising seconds later the car hit the barrier, turned a couple of somersaults, and came to a crashing halt upside down on its roof. I screeched to a halt on the hard shoulder, together with a few other drivers who had miraculously missed all the rolling and swerving. I was trembling in shock, but desperate to go and help Ken. We all rushed over to the overturned car. I was fighting like a woman possessed to try to get Ken out, and petrol was gushing out of the burst fuel tank. But his right leg was badly trapped and it was hopeless.

The emergency services were there within a few minutes, though of course it seemed ages, and the firemen freed Ken and helped the ambulance people to get him on to a stretcher. I walked back to my Escort through a firework show of flashing blue lights and followed the ambulance to the hospital. None of it seemed real.

In casualty they were ready and waiting, and immediately went into action.

I was shown into a waiting room and given a hot, sweet cup of tea.

The wait seemed endless. I smelled all the familiar smells associated with hospitals, and watched the white coats of the doctors flapping around their knees as they walked to and fro. I remember thinking how dignified the nurses were in the starched aprons and frilly caps, but it was all like a dream. Or rather, a nightmare. How was it possible to be so happy one moment and so completely devastated the next?

Eventually a nice young doctor came to see me. He looked absolutely exhausted, fair hair flopping over his face, shoulders sagging.

"I'm sorry," he said. "We did everything we could. We tried to get his heart going again, but his injuries were very severe. I'm afraid your friend has died."

I mooched around for the next couple of days in a trance. Nothing around me seemed to register. Nothing mattered. Nothing made any sense any more.

There had to be a post-mortem and an inquest of course, and Steve Allen, Ken's solicitor, who was also his friend, looked after all that. The body was finally released and Steve made all the funeral arrangements. I just sat through it all like a zombie, completely unable to take in what had happened.

Life without Ken was going to be horribly empty. He was such a necessary person, so alive, so good, never vain or boastful of the success he had made of life. He was just a nice guy, one of the best.

But eventually of course, I had to go back to work.

Leadenhall Street on a wet Monday morning looked as dreary as I felt. Walking into an empty office and seeing Ken's empty desk was going to be the hardest part of all. No cheery greeting, no "Good morning Val, what have we got exciting in the post today?"

The work had piled up and I knew there was no alternative but to make a start on tackling it, but every envelope seemed to weigh a ton, its contents meaningless. I played with the papers. There seemed no point in doing anything with them, ever again.

The day wore miserably on, and I seemed to be getting nowhere fast. I had constant interruptions all morning, the telephone flashing incessantly. I have to rely on the flashing as I can't hear a phone from any distance away.

Out of the corner of my eye I saw its light yet again. I breathed a deep sigh and flicked the switch. Joyce. She apologized for troubling me again, but said that she thought it was important, as it was Steve on the line.

"Thank you, Joyce" I answered, a little wearily, picking up the phone. "Hello Steve, what can I do for you?"

"Valerie, how are you?"

"Fair" I replied. "Bearing up."

His voice softened. "Look Val" he went on. "Do you think you could possibly pop in and see me one day this week, or better still could we have lunch?" I hesitated, wondering how I was going to fit it in with all the additional work, and then realised that Steve would not have asked me if it wasn't something important.

"Of course, Steve, I should like that."

"Would Wednesday suit you, say about one o'clock at the Palmerston?"

I flicked through my diary. "Fine" I answered "Bye for now".

The day ground on in the same dead way, and I finally joined the mad rush home from Liverpool Street, not even bothering to try and dodge the stampede of feet, umbrellas and briefcases.

Racehorses don't know how lucky they are. Owners and trainers don't make them travel on trains packed like sardines, as we have to.

Digging a few people with my elbows, I managed to turn to the back page of The Standard to see what had won at Warwick. Nothing very exciting there, but then nothing seemed very exciting any more.

The front page of the paper was full of depressing world news, and the all-too-familiar muggings of old people. Was it always going to feel like this? Would life ever be worth living again?

CHAPTER TWO

The Palmerston was a classy restaurant, patronised by the cream of the city. I just wished as we were shown to our table that I had been more in the mood to enjoy it. Steve looked very smart and gave me a warm welcome. But there was something anxious him; a tension in the air.

We ordered, and Steve came straight to the point. "Valerie, there's something you might not have known about Ken. He was a Barnardo's boy. Like me."

I hadn't known that, and his words shook me. Yet when I came to think about it, Ken had said suspiciously little about his early days. He had always given me the impression that he had had a happy childhood, but he had never given me any detail.

"He's left the bulk of his estate to them. Not surprising, really. They were the people who looked after him so well when he was young."

I could understand that. It was just what I would have expected of Ken. He had always shown his appreciation for the smallest act of kindness bestowed upon him.

If that news had shaken me, Steve's next words really bowled me over.

"But I've got another surprise' he said. 'He left something to you. His most prized possession. Val, he's left you Music Adored.'

I stared in disbelief.

'He's also left you enough money to pay for training fees and expenses."

To say I was staggered would be the understatement of the year. I went through so many emotions that I didn't know which one hit me first.

The first, I think, was the thought that Ken had really loved me. He must have done to have left me what he valued most in life, the horse he had named after his lifelong love of music. Then sadness, that now I would never be able to let him know just how much he meant to me. And after that, joy, such unbelievable and overwhelming joy, that I had actually become an owner.

It had always been my dream to have a horse of my own, and I could never begin to imagine what it would be like, but the idea that Music Adored was to be mine was a little too much to take in.

Anyway, when all the joy, sadness and heart-throbbing began to subside and I had started to come back down to earth, I realised I hadn't asked Steve all the important questions. He had been so patient while I had been going through this emotional upheaval, quietly getting on with his drink and obviously realising that it was a lot for me to take in.

"What was the result of the inquest, Steve?" I felt I couldn't go to the Coroner's Court and go through all the traumatic details again. Somewhere along the line I had just taken it for granted that the car must have been faulty, or Ken had suddenly been taken ill.

"Accidental death Val, what we thought."

"Accidental death? Oh come on Steve! Why? Was he ill?"

"Not according to the post mortem. He was in perfect health until his car hit the barrier."

"Then it was the car. What was it, a burst tyre? Steering?"

"Not according to the insurance company. Their bloke gave it a very thorough inspection. He couldn't find anything wrong with it."

Steve put his glass on the table and beckoned the waiter for a refill.

"Will you have another, Val?"

"No thanks Steve. I've got a lot of work on this afternoon. I'd better keep a clear head."

I was feeling very agitated. I thought back to the night at Stratford when Ken had become distraught about some men we had passed in the car park. Had there been some kind of cover-up?

"Look Steve, let's look at this in a logical way. The accident must have been caused by something. What did they say at the inquest?"

"The only thing they could put it down to was that Ken might have dozed off for a few seconds, or lost concentration. People do nod off when they're driving you know, it happens all the time."

"Not with people like Ken."

I couldn't believe that. He was an expert driver, and very conscious of his responsibilities towards other people. I would never be able to believe that Ken, of all people, had died through his own carelessness.

The lunch was so good and so beautifully presented that I found myself eating properly for the first time in weeks. What's more, I was actually enjoying it. The food and the wine was making me feel much more relaxed and less disorientated. I decided there and then that as soon as I got home I would start trying to sort things out in a rational way. I would go through every detail and try and make some sense of the whole bewildering affair.

Steve had mentioned that Ken had recently updated his will, which was strange for a man of his age; something was obviously worrying him. What – or who?

The change had to do with the horse. It seemed the will stated very clearly that Music Adored was to remain with her present trainer, Simon Galloway. Simon was young, but he had had a successful record so far. He was a great believer in modern techniques. Ken was insistent that the horse should never be returned to the trainer who had bred her, Amanda Neale-Adamson. I had already decided that I would continue to race in Ken's colours, blue and claret - he was a West Ham fan. It felt like the least I could do.

We left the restaurant and walked down the steps into Bishopsgate. Steve said he would be in touch. There were papers to be signed, decisions to be made.

I fought my way through the usual scrum from Liverpool Street and put on all the heating; it was a cold and miserable day. I made myself a coffee, thankful that I didn't have to prepare any food. Then I snuggled down into the sofa and started to think.

Ever since the accident I had been going over those last few terrible minutes in my mind again and again. And still I hadn't a clue why Ken had really died.

The Anglo-Catholic church I attend was looking more lovely than ever on the Sunday. We had celebrated our Patronial Festival that week and the devoted ladies had cleaned the church, polished the brass and arranged the flowers to perfection.

I dipped my finger in the holy water and crossed my forehead as I entered, then made my way to my usual pew down the front in anticipation of our guest preacher not having a beard, and that I would, therefore, be able to lip-read at least a little of what he was preaching.

It had never occurred to me that I was particularly religious, but I had always thought that High Mass was one of the most moving and beautiful things in the world and I had always enjoyed meeting, once a week at least, the people I had loved and respected all my life. It was all so familiar to me, and yet it felt so strange.

The priest gracefully glided towards the altar in his colourful vestments and the sacristan and servers busily carried out their various duties, remembering to genuflect as they passed from one side of the chancel to the other. With the sung responses and the overpowering small of incense, it all cast a powerful spell.

I must have nodded off and started dreaming. I came to with a start as the man beside me extended his hand. "Peace be with you," he was saying. Peace was the one thing I wanted more than anything else, but was unable to find. I was confused, unsettled. I felt as if I was on the outside looking in.

When mass was over and the congregation had gone over to the hall for coffee and gossip, I went over to the Shrine of Our Lady and lit a candle for Ken. I knelt before the Holy Mother, desperately wanting to say a special prayer. But somehow, it just wouldn't come. I couldn't find the right words.

Even so, as I knelt there, I gradually began to feel serenity creeping back into my body. Peace was indeed beginning to be with me again. My thoughts were sorting themselves out, finding their way into the right slots. Although the right prayer wouldn't come to my lips, I felt that the Holy Mother was getting the message, and that she would pray for me.

It was at that moment, in the peace and serenity of the church, that it came into my mind that the 'accident' had not been an accident at all.

Could someone have deliberately tried to put the BMW and its driver out of action? But it would have to have been a case of mistaken identity. Everybody who knew Ken liked him. Surely they must have mistaken the car and the driver for somebody else, someone they wished to dispose of. Ken had surely just been caught up in someone else's vendetta.

As these thoughts wheeled round and round in my head, I began to feel there had to be a reason for the car to go out of control the way it did. I would never be able to accept the view of the coroner that Ken's death was accidental. Kneeling there before the Holy Mother, I felt I was being given an inner strength to somehow go out and try to get to the bottom of this mystery.

Above all, I felt I owed it to Ken, in return for all he had done for me. He had been great to me when alive, and now, although my dearest wish would be to have had him alive and well, he had left me what he prized most, his beloved Music Adored. For this honour alone, I was determined to do my best to prove that the accident had not been Ken's fault. I knew it was not just instinct pressing me on. My whole body was screaming out that there was something phoney about the whole affair.

When I walked out into the autumn sunshine, it was like coming out of a thick fog. I had made up my mind to do something about the situation, and already I felt better, much, much better.

CHAPTER THREE

The first thing to do was to get the car checked over. Dick, my late husband, had been in the motor trade all his life and often used to test-drive cars on the tracks for the brake and tyre companies. He had known a lot of mechanics. One of them, a chap called Bob Andrews, had written to me when Dick died, saying he would always pop over and give my car a service for me. I hadn't taken him up on that, but I still had all the letters and cards I had received at the time, and thought it worth the price of a stamp to see if he was still living at the same address.

He was, and he phoned me a couple of days later. He said he had retired, but he was delighted to have the opportunity to get his hands on something other than the routine jobs he was now doing for his friends and relations. I put him in the picture as to what had happened and what had been said at the inquest. The insurance company gave permission for an independent inspection, and I faxed over the details to Bob that night. He came back to me the following day, suggesting we meet for a drink at a little pub in the city just off Broad Street, where we would be able to talk without interruption.

It was good to see this cheery little chap again. He was so genuine and unassuming, and by all accounts he had been an excellent mechanic to one of the top racing drivers. I knew I could rely on what he had to tell me. But it was not the enlightenment I had hoped for.

"I've gone over that BMW with a fine-tooth comb, Valerie. Apart from the crash damage, it's sound. There's nothing, absolutely nothing, that might have caused the crash."

This was not easy for me to accept. I had been so sure that the insurance man had missed something. After all, he was checking out cars every day of the week; surely one was very much like another to him. But if Bob said there was nothing wrong with the car, I had to accept his word for it.

It was good to see Bob again. He really was a dear, positively refusing to accept any payment or expenses for the past two days. He said how much he had respected and liked Dick in the old days and how Dick would always go out of his way to get spare parts that were tricky to find. He said the boys used to call Dick the kingpin king.

All this made me even more determined to investigate further, but what the next step was going to be I had no idea. All I could do was play it by ear. Perhaps Steve would have some suggestions to make. I would have to give him a ring.

I had had the most uneasy feeling since the night before the accident. Ken had been sent a couple of tickets for the first night at the Theatre Royal, Stratford, East London, of a play called Stiff Options. He was Vice President of the Waltham Forest Brass Band, and they were going to play to welcome the celebrities.

The theatre had been completely redecorated and refurnished, and the management had opened their doors to the gentlemen of the press and the world of showbiz. The streets of East London were awash with Rollses and Porsches, and the East Londoners had turned out in force in their good-hearted way to welcome them.

Ken's band were looking very smart in their blue and black uniforms. They were seated in the paved Gerry Raffles Square outside the theatre, ready to strike up with songs from the shows as the guests and press began to arrive. As the crowds began to thicken, the atmosphere started to warm up. Simon, the Musical Director, was getting well into his stride, urging the band to give it everything they'd got. It wasn't long before the crowds lining the grass banks and flanking the square were singing the good old tunes, and it only took If You Knew Susie to get them dancing, the youngsters allowing the old 'uns to show them the way. In no time at all people were dancing all around the square.

Every so often there was a pause and a rousing cheer as a favourite star arrived, but some of the celebrities were only inside long enough to grab a drink and a snack before they returned to the outside fun. A call then came for them to take their seats, as the curtain was due to go up in five minutes.

The West End had come to the East End, and it turned out to be the best knees-up since the Royal Wedding. Like everyone else that night, Ken was having problems finding a parking space, so he suggested we should make for the multi-storey car park over the shopping centre. We were so happy, the festive mood had captured us, and hand in hand, laughing together at such silly little things, we were making our way back to the theatre.

As we reached level 1 of the car park we saw two men who appeared to be engaged in intense conversation. One of them I recognized as a man called Chopper. He was the leader of a bunch of crooks and had got his nickname after he had three fingers of his left hand chopped off by a rival gang. His picture appeared with monotonous regularity in the papers. He had opened a stall in Walthamstow High Street after his wife had divorced him because he had lost the licence of the pub her father had set them up in when they married. Now he had to get the money for the life he had become accustomed to by running a protection racket round the East London markets.

I could only see the back of the man he was talking to, but Ken must have known who it was as his mood appeared to change from that moment. Whoever it was, it seemed to keep his thoughts pretty well occupied all evening. He tried hard not to let it show, but I was very sensitive to his moods and I became more and more worried as the night wore on.

The play was by John Flanagan and Andrew McCulloch, whose TV work included, among much else, The Sweeney and The Heavy Mob. Never in my wildest dreams could I have visualised that my own life was soon to unfold as if they had written the plot.

We set off for home in near silence.

"What's up Ken, it's not like you not to enjoy a good joke?" I ventured.

"Of course I enjoyed it, it's been a fantastic evening," he said, brushing my cheek. "Goodnight Val, God bless."

"Goodnight Ken. Please make sure you make it to Kempton tomorrow, I'll look out for you."

If only I had been able to.

CHAPTER FOUR

Wetherby's were most helpful in supplying all the information a new owner has to know. Music Adored was re-registered in my name. The boys and girls at the office had had a whipround for my birthday and came up with a smart new blanket for her, the very latest, with my initials beautifully embroidered in the corner. I was overwhelmed by their kindness and thoughtfulness, and had to make my way quickly over to the table to get busy with the little savouries, cakes and wine that made birthdays an excuse for indulgence. The tears were splashing on to the priceless little bits of smoked salmon, and everyone was being kind enough to pretend not to notice. This I would treasure always, and they knew it.

Quite naturally, they had all taken a keen interest in the boss's horses. In fact, they had formed their own fan club, roping in their boyfriends, girlfriends, husbands and wives; they put a pound in the kitty every week and when one of the horses was running at a Saturday meeting they hired a coach, took plenty of eats and drinks with them and made it a good day out.

Thanks to the rest of the staff the in-tray was looking much healthier, so the following Tuesday I decided to take a day's leave. I jumped into the Escort and drove down to Surrey to make myself known at the Simon Galloway Stables.

I liked Simon straight away. He was a nice lad and I could see why Ken had insisted on the horse remaining there. He clearly knew what he was doing and was committed to doing his best for Music.

Cleanliness and efficiency were apparent everywhere. The staff seemed to get on well with each other and with the 'guvnor'. Simon told me that they grew all their own food on the farm - hay, straw, oats, with plenty of vitamins and minerals, and molasses. It looked like a thick black treacle to me, but he said it was full of iron and a very good appetiser, with linseed, bran and beet pulp.

An extraordinary feeling crept over me as we made our way toward Music Adored's box. I was finding it hard to realise that she was actually mine, and although of course I would have given the world to have Ken alive and well again, it was all so thrilling. I knew Ken would want me to enjoy every moment and not be sad in any way, but it was not easy to separate the two emotions. They would get mixed up however I tried to keep them apart. One thing that made me feel really good was that Music was being cared for in such a good and loving home.

As we strolled on, Simon told me that at times he put the horses into the field to be with the sheep and cows and other farm animals. It sounded almost like a fairy story.

"They all get on so well together" he said. "They really enjoy each other's company. It makes them feel at home, part of the family."

I could see why he was becoming so successful. He obviously cared very much for all the animals and naturally wanted to do his best for them.

As the first lot came from the gallops we watched them come in to get ready to be hosed down.

"When the ground's hard with frost I like to take them down to Camber Sands near Rye for a gallop" he said. "If it's not too cold I let them have a little paddle. They love a gallop and the sea water's good for their legs."

It must have been quite hard work, loading them, driving them down and attending to all their needs, but Simon made it sound like a British Rail Breakaway Day. I thought of Music galloping along Camber Sands and how beautiful she must look.

"I don't believe in entering horses in National Hunt races too young, Mrs. Elphick" he confided. "I think five or six is plenty young enough to start racing. That way they should get to their peak when they're nine or ten."

* * * * * * * *

Among the bills in the Monday morning post was a long, official-looking envelope from Steve's company, full of legal documents. He had put a personal note inside suggesting he would call the following evening, when he would explain the various papers to me. I phoned him to say that Tuesday was my night at the judo club, but I normally arrived home around nine-fifteen and had a late supper. I said I'd be delighted if he would join me then, if it wasn't too late for him.

Before I left home I put some chicken breast fillets and a few sliced vegetables in a cook-in sauce in the oven and speared some jacket potatoes to go with it, leaving it to cook slowly. When I opened the door on my return, the smell that greeted me was gorgeous. It was just as well that Steve arrived almost immediately after me, or there would probably have been very little left for him. This judo lark made one very hungry. At the little bakery round the corner from where I worked, they made delicious apple pies, so light they just melted in the mouth, and topped with cream they finished off a very nice little supper.

The coffee was perking nicely, and to give myself a bit of Dutch courage I poured two brandies. Now I felt better able to approach Steve again about Ken's accident.

"Look Steve, I know you think I've got a vivid imagination, but I can't shake off this feeling about Ken" I began. "I know he was bothered about something the night before he died. I don't know if I'll ever be able to prove it, but I am sure it wasn't an accident."

Steve was a bit stuffy. "I think, my dear, that you really must try and put your thoughts in another direction. You're very upset, and it's quite understandable that you should try to find someone to blame. I'd be the last to be disrespectful to old Ken, but we do all make mistakes at times. It really would be much easier if you could accept that. Look, if there was anything to be suspicious about, the police would have detected it. Anyway, you've had the car checked yourself."

It was becoming clear that Steve was not going to help.

"OK Steve, I know what you're saying, I can see you think I'm going crazy."

"I don't think you're crazy Val, but there just isn't a shred of evidence that anything was wrong with the car. You can't start a private enquiry just on instinct, it's too expensive these days anyway. Ken hadn't mentioned anything to me about any problems he was having. Not that he would of course, I only dealt with his personal legal affairs. Any proceedings relating to the business would have to go through Lloyds' Legal Department."

As I listened and looked at his soft, earnest eyes, I began to realise how fond of him I was becoming. He really did care how I felt. I didn't know then that the feeling was reciprocal. It was hurting Steve to see me tearing myself to pieces like this.

Without Ken, the normal smooth running of the office had gone to pot. All the staff were doing their best to cope with the additional work, but things were beginning to get a bit out of hand. We were going to have to do some reorganising very soon.

On the Wednesday evening I decided to stay late to try and catch up with a few of the more pressing problems. Once I had got stuck in, the time just simply slid away.

As anyone with a hearing problem will know, it makes you more sensitive to movement and vibrations – rather as blind people have better hearing. That's how I must suddenly have known, without hearing a sound, that there was someone in the outer office.

At first, I thought it was probably one of the security guards checking everything was OK, but a security guard would not be opening drawers and filing cabinets. Somebody was looking for something, and the way he was going about it he knew what he was doing.

I sat up and gave it all my attention. I was watching for any change in the light, waiting for any sense that would tell me what was happening. Very soon the intruder was going to discover that there was nothing worth finding out there, and in all probability he'd be making his way into the inner office.

I forced my breathing back to a more steady rhythm and tried to stop my heart hammering so loudly they'd hear it in the street. I said a silent thank you to Mick the trainer, who had had me sweating my guts out for an hour every Tuesday and Thursday doing press-ups, squat thrusts and break-falls.

I knew I was no Brian Jacks - it had taken me seven years and twenty-one gradings just to get a green belt - but I reckoned that unless the bloke in the next room was going to turn out to be a black belt, I might just be able to put up some sort of show.

The only reason I had gone in for judo in the first place was because I enjoyed my food too much, and it had caused a bit of a weight problem. But this was the first time I had had occasion to be thankful for it.

I was so scared I wasn't sure I'd be able to stand up, let alone disable an attacker, but my brain was working double time to try and figure out the best way to tackle him. If he came in from the door behind me I could go for an ippon seoi-nage, which meant grabbing him round the neck while he was still behind me and throwing him forward over my head. If on the other hand he came in from the door at the side, it would have to be a tomoe-nage - I would have to grab him from the front and roll backwards on the floor, taking him with me, throwing him behind me. Or perhaps a tai-otoshi would be better, bouncing him off the hip.

I was praying he didn't know judo himself. It's all very well being thrown by a professional instructor on to two thousand quid's worth of beautifully sprung mat. It wouldn't be so much fun coming down on top of one of the filing cabinets.

As it happened, I didn't have any more time to think about it. Suddenly I became aware of a shadow behind me. As soon as I saw it I performed the tai-otoshi. He was a big bloke, but he was quite unprepared. He was on his feet in a trice and running for the door. I chased him all the way out into Lime Street. He must have been quite a heavy guy, fifteen or sixteen stone, but he was a fast mover.

The alarm was raised and a search made immediately, but there was no sign of him. He had known his way around - must have been a professional. But what could he have wanted to steal? No large sums of money or valuables were ever kept at the office, only files, papers, information...

Information, that's what he must have been after. When all the excitement was over and I began to turn it over in my mind, I wondered if there could possibly be any connection with Ken's accident. Could he have come up with something, then someone had rumbled it and put him out of action?

That was it - there had to be a connection. One thing I was sure of was that the guy in the office was not the man who had been talking to Chopper at Stratford the night of the play. Their builds were dead opposite.

I phoned Steve - not just to say, "I told you so", but because I really needed a friend to talk to about it. He suggested that we should try and take a look around the East End to see if we could find the man Ken and I had seen in the car park, the man who I felt sure had something to do with what had happened to him.

We agreed on a pub crawl. We'd start at the Sparrows, the pub nearest the place where we'd seen Chopper and the other man, then explore from there.

"What are you drinking, Val?" said Steve at the bar of the Sparrows.

"I'm the one who knows the area. I'll stick with tonic water and do the driving."

We wound our way through an assortment of Kings - Alfred, George and Harold – followed by a few Queens, Arms and Princes, Albert, George and William. There were some lords - Henniker, Clyde and Palmerston - thrown in. Very patriotic, the Cockneys. They also seem to be very fond of green, judging by the Green Man, Green Gates and Green Dragon. Finally, as it seemed appropriate, The Chevy Chase.

Fifteen tonics down, and there hadn't been a sign of anyone who looked remotely like Chopper's friend.

This was not altogether surprising, as all the pubs had been glamourised in the past few years, with subdued lighting, usually red, orange or green. It was difficult to recognise your best friend, let alone someone you didn't know.

I had always thought of Steve as a bit of a stuffed shirt. If I'd known he and Ken were ex-Barnardo boys, I might have understood more readily how hard it must have been for them both to have reached such high levels in their respective chosen professions. But tonight was different. He was beginning to let his hair down a little, to become more human. He was also making a few mistakes, which was unusual.

It was inevitable, as a practising lawyer, that Steve must have had to get involved with investigations from time to time, but he would always employ solicitors' agents for the job. He himself had yet to learn the most elementary rudiments of investigation.

Trick one: order a gin and tonic, fill the glass to the brim with the tonic, take one sip, then either knock it over or give the nearest rubber plant a treat. The easiest way to detect where those on the wanted list hang out is to study the plants. They are usually well knackered. You need to be alert when you're on a manhunt.

I made a fairly neat job of parking Steve's car in his garage and cleverly disengaged myself from attempt at a goodnight kiss. Then I managed to catch a cabbie's eye to take me home.

CHAPTER FIVE

On the Saturday morning I was looking forward to a day's racing at Newbury. The Teasmade came up with my cuppa just as Richard the newsboy was popping the Racing Post through the letter-box.

This was sheer luxury - to sit up in bed with a cup of tea to absorb and compare the knowledge of the experts. I had so often said that I would rather go without lunch than give up my Racing Post, or in the old days the Sporting Life, and this was the one day of the week when I could take my time and digest the various opinions, together with those of The Scout on the Express and Captain Heath of the Mail. Not that I would necessarily back the tips they gave.

Better to back a favourite that wins than an outsider that loses, the old hands used to say, but I very rarely made my choice until I had seen the horses in the parade ring and watched them go down to the start. A jockey can easily lose a race by the way he takes the horse down to the start, so it is very important to watch that.

You need to know about form of course, but I try not to get too involved. I prefer to rely on my own instincts and to see how the horses look and behave in the paddock. It had not let me down too badly in the past, although I must confess that there had been many times when I had leaned over the rail of the parade ring and tried to lip-read snippets of conversation between trainers, owners and jockeys, which sometimes had helped me reach a final decision. There must have been something in it, because I always noticed that when I watched racing on television, I could never seem to find the winners as I did at the course.

My friends pulled my leg, of course. They said I did better than they did with racing on television, because I couldn't hear what the tipsters were saying.

Tipsters have always come in for a lot of criticism, rightly so in some cases, but the game would come to an end if they knew every winner. In the old days, when they sent their 'certainties' by post, the system was to split the country into however many horses were running in the race. If there were eight runners, then a map of the British Isles was split into eight sections, with a different horse tipped for each section, so someone, somewhere, had to win, and they lived in hope that the population as a whole each received their fair share of winners. It didn't work out that way of course, and then the letters started to pour in - "You couldn't tip your grandmother out of bed" etc.

I well remember as a youngster the laughter and fun we had when the great Prince Monoloulo, such a colourful figure on the course, would come home with my father after a day's racing for a meal or a drink. They would either be recalling the praises and adulation that had been rained on him if he had found a winner, or the various suggestions as to how he could dispose of his tips, if they had failed. It's much more sophisticated today, but it was more fun then.

It was very often possible then to lose money without having a bet, thanks to the pickpockets on the course and three-card tricksters on the trains. Very often when a new face appeared on the trains they were broke before they reached the course. If they managed to escape that hazard they would more than likely pull a wallet out of a back pocket, bulging with notes, to place a bet on the first race. The wallet would be gone by the second race.

This was the weekday occupation of the boys who did Petticoat Lane on a Sunday. It was said that they would nick a gentleman's handkerchief out of his pocket at one end of the Lane and sell it back to him at the other end.

It was all kids' stuff compared to the high technology of the crooks of today, but nonetheless it made them a tidy penny or two. If they invested it in property it wouldn't be long before the three-card tricksters, along with the bookies' runners of the pre-betting office days, could live in comfortable retirement, very often spending the best part of the winter in the Bahamas soaking up the sun. They could sit back in their Parker Knolls and muse over the battle of wits they used to have with the local coppers who tried to book them for taking bets.

One East End copper was very aggrieved that the runners always managed to outrun him. He was determined to book them, so one day he borrowed a barrow, dressed up in his old togs, rolled up his sleeves and put on a choker and cap. Then he paraded the streets as a rag-and-bone man, thinking his disguise was complete. Of course he hadn't fooled them one bit. As he made his rounds they piled his cart high with all the old rubbish they could lay their hands on - old tables, chairs, rags, any old sinks, bins, with a few rotten tomatoes thrown in for good measure.

I had a leisurely bath instead of the usual quick shower, put on my comfortable trousers, suede jacket and 'racing shoes', swung my binoculars over my shoulder and was ready for the "off". It did occur to me that Steve might not be feeling his usual self, and I thought it better to give him a ring before I left. I really had enjoyed my night out with him, although it had not brought any immediate results.

Brurr... brurr ... brurr... no answer. Then someone picked up. I turned my amplifier on full blast. Perhaps I was not hearing him.

"Yes?"

"Steve, how are you this morning?" He sounded terrible.

"Oh Val... leave me. For about a fortnight."

"What's up, Steve?"

"My head feels as if there are ten little men with hammers inside it, all in competition to see who can bang the loudest."

"Oh you poor dear, shall I come round and fix you something? Coffee and an aspirin?"

"No thanks Val, I'll manage."

I guessed Steve wouldn't want me to see him right now. He always looked so well turned-out.

"Any more of your bright ideas Val, and one solicitor's agent will be minus a client" he said. "In future I think I might do a little investigating of my own, I might even enjoy it. There must be quite a bit of satisfaction turning something up. I'll have to start with the easy ones though and work my way up. You've dropped me right in at the deep end. If this Chopper bloke has anything to do with it, he knows how to handle himself."

The traffic was light, being Saturday, and I was making good time to Newbury. I found the winner of the first. Simon had finished saddling up the only horse he had running at Newbury that afternoon, and noticed me as he was leading the horse into the parade ring.

"Would you join me for a drink after the fourth, Mrs. Elphick? I'd like to have a word with you before you go."

My heart felt as if it had dropped to my tatty old shoes. Was something the matter with Music Adored? I was silently sending up a little prayer - "please let her be all right."

"Yes I'd like to" I said. "Shall I meet you in the bar?"

"OK. And by the way, good luck."

Simon's horse won comfortably, and he notched up another winner for the season.

It must have been one of the longest hours ever. Normally there was hardly time to get everything in between races. Putting on bets, drawing winnings, catching a quick cup of tea, and the part I enjoyed most of all, watching the horses in the parade ring, trying to pick up little snippets of information.

By the time Simon arrived I had already ordered a coffee for myself, but he insisted I should have a brandy in it, as the afternoon was turning nippy. In my state of mind, this suggestion made me feel even worse. I felt sure he was trying to soften some sort of blow, and I could only think of Music Adored, so his words as he tipped the brandy into my coffee took me by surprise.

"I had a young fella down at the yard the other day, said he was a reporter, asking a lot of questions about you" he said.

I couldn't believe it. "Asking questions about me? How could anyone possibly want to know anything about me?"

People were continuously interrupting us, wanting to shake Simon's hand. Obviously they were the ones who had backed his horse.

"I thought it was a bit odd at the time" he went on. "I've never seen this chap before, certainly not at any of the meetings, and they usually make themselves known to us, particularly when they want some information for a write-up in the next day's paper. Normally it's the horses the questions are all about, but this one kept asking me about you, what you did, your connection with racing and so on. Naturally I told him I don't discuss owners with reporters. It also struck me as odd that he seemed to be completely uninterested in Music Adored, particularly as he said he was from your local paper. I would have thought it would have been better for him to have contacted you locally. I thought I had better let you know, put you on your guard if he should call to see you."

"Thanks Simon, I'm glad you told me. How is Music?"

"Fine. When the ground's right we'll enter her for another race. I'll be in touch. By the way, I should give the paper a ring if I were you, see if they did send somebody down."

First thing Monday morning I phoned the Gazette. The girl who answered sounded about nineteen. I could visualise her immediately - a miniskirt that looked like a pelmet, dyed hair, loads of mascara, ridiculously long fingernails. Her name had to be Tracy.

"Could I speak to the editor, please?"

Tracy was horrified - the big boss? Certainly not.

"I'll put you through to his secretary" she said. She transferred me to a reporter, who then transferred me to another reporter, who then had me put through to the sports section, and finally back to the secretary. I was getting up tight now.

"Please let me have a quick word with the editor" I pleaded. To my surprise, it worked.

"I doubt if any of my reporters have ever heard of a horse called Music Adored, let alone its owner" he assured me. "No, we certainly didn't send a reporter to the stables, and besides it would not be our policy to ask personal details of a third party. We'd have contacted you direct."

"Of course, thank you for speaking to me."

I had a busy morning ahead, and for the time being at least I had to concentrate on what I was doing and put this strange incident out of my mind. Nevertheless, during the day it kept floating back from time to time.

I contacted Steve. "Look Val" he said. "I think perhaps it would be as well if I had a word with the agent I normally call on for this sort of thing. This is more in his line."

"No, please don't do that Steve, it will only involve a lot of expense and there's so little information we can give him at this stage."

I didn't tell Steve that I felt in my heart that I had to be involved personally, as a sort of thank you to Ken. No doubt the initiative that was spurring me on was really revenge. If someone had been directly responsible for Ken's death, I wanted to see them pay for it. I might have been an amateur, but I certainly had the incentive.

I decided that the next day I would start cross-checking all the details of the horses underwritten to the firm and try to discover if a fraudulent claim had been made. I checked, re-checked and double-checked. I had all the veterinary certificates verified, and I paid special attention to all the markings.

I checked two Australian horses particularly carefully. They had similar markings, but one cost $125,000 and the other $35,000. A claim had been paid out for the first horse, but it was later discovered that a horse entered in the name of the second horse for a race at Melbourne was the one which was supposed to have died. The case was with the legal department. But I could find no connection at all with Chopper and his associates.

Surely there must be something here I was missing, if it was important enough for an intruder to want it? I would just have to press on. It was probably staring me in the face. I just wasn't seeing it.

CHAPTER SIX

On the Saturday I got my usual flash of lights from the paper boy and rushed down to pick up the Racing Post. Among the letters on the mat was one which bore the stamp of the Evening Standard. Could it be?

My fingers trembled so much that I had one hell of a job getting the thing open. Once I did I was hit by that beautiful, wonderful word – "Congratulations!"

I had won a competition sponsored by United Racecourses Ltd and would receive a champagne lunch, a grandstand seat to see the Sandown Salver, the world's top jockeys competing in the Great Britain v. USA jockeys' "rubber" match at Sandown Park, together with fourteen months' free membership at the course. I felt I was going to burst with joy. I had known I could do it, but I hadn't really expected to.

Although National Hunt racing had always been my favourite I had always taken a keen interest in the flat, and knew very well that I had answered the questions correctly. It was the slogan that had had me worried – I had to say something pithy about Sandown Park. I had just put what I believed to be true, that it was well-designed, attractive, sporty and very efficient. The judges must have been satisfied.

So instead of the usual Saturday morning business of spreading all the papers around and picking out winners, I decided for this very important day that I really should invest in a new pair of 'racing shoes'. It has always amazed me how the ladies manage Royal Ascot in their fancy shoes. I always preferred to put on comfortable togs and feel free and easy to enjoy the racing, but for this day my feet were going to have to suffer.

As it happened it was all so exciting that I hardly noticed I was tottering around on high heels. Some sharp-eyed person at the local Gazette had seen my name in the Evening Standard when the winners were announced and had turned up at my house to take a picture of me sticking my Members' Car Park ticket on the windscreen of my car. Then the photographer, together with a few of the neighbours, waved me on my way, all wishing me a lucky and happy day. They knew I had had a bit of a rough time of late and they seemed genuinely pleased to see me looking so happy.

I got to the course around 11 o'clock and was told to make my way to the secretary's office. From there I was escorted over to Members and taken up to the banqueting suite. Here I was introduced to 'Falcon' of the Standard, who began introducing me to all the people around. I knew some of the faces, but I also knew I was going to make a complete fool of myself, because the lighting in the bar was not suitable for lip-reading and it is only possible to lip-read one-to-one.

It was time for me to confess. I took the Falcon aside.

"I know I should have mentioned this to you before, but I don't hear" I said.

"You what?"

"I don't hear."

He turned to the racing manager and said, "we've gone to all this trouble and she's not going to hear a bloody thing!"

"I do lip-read" I replied.

"What was the greatest horse ever?"

"Arkle, in my book."

"You'll do."

"Please just don't expect me to be able to communicate with all the people at the table - I can only manage one-to-one".

At noon the first champagne cork popped, and it went on flowing all afternoon, as freely as the never-ending racing tales which racegoers always enjoy telling and listening to. The atmosphere was electric. Everybody who was anybody in racing circles was lunching in Members that day, and even the most experienced of racing people were getting excited about this very special day.

Sandown was looking its best. Always lovely, it seemed now to have a special sparkle, and after twenty days of rain (it had been the wettest month of the year so far), I was not the only one on my knees praying for a nice day. The organisers needed a gate of at least 7000 to break even.

The jockeys arrived, all in their team jackets. The British team were sporting the Union Jack, and the Americans the Stars and Stripes. ITV pulled out all the stops, and sent a complete team - John Oaksey, Brough Scott and Derek Thompson were all there, as there were so many people to be interviewed.

The splendid lunch was over at last and we were all preparing to get down to the main business of the day - the racing. Could anything be better than this? Good company, good food, and now we were leaning on the rails of the paddock anticipating good, competitive racing.

Finding the winner of the first two races was not easy, but who cared? There was plenty of time to put things right before the end of the day. The two-forty-five was one mile six furlongs, and the start was in front of the grandstand. I loved being out there, jostling among the bookmakers, comparing the prices, and feeling great if I could get in at a price one point above what most of the bookies were laying. I was just thinking that I would walk over to see the horses go into the stalls, when suddenly, there he was, right in front of me. Chopper.

Well I'll be blowed. All that time scanning the East End pubs and here he was served up on a plate, so to speak. But what could I do now that I had found him? I could hardly confront him without a shred of evidence that he was mixed up in anything. I didn't even know not what – it was just my feminine instinct doing overtime.

I pushed through the crowds making their way up to the stands and took the lift up to the second floor. If I hadn't already lost my target this would be a good vantage point from which to keep an eye on him, see if he made any contacts. I had a good pair of glasses - I needed them, as I was unable to hear the commentary. From the Members' dining hall I could get an all-round view. One side of the room covered the course, the other the paddock and the unsaddling enclosure.

I kept my eyes glued to Chopper for the best part of the afternoon, up until I was led over to have my picture taken with Lester Piggott and Willie Carson. Lester led the English team, and Willie scored the most points that day. The final score was Britain 40, USA 26.

I was now given the opportunity to ask Derek Thompson if he would allow me to nominate him as "Golden Lips of the Year" for sports fans. He is easy to lip-read and has such good expressions. He won of course, because I got all my mates to vote for him.

The photo was in the next day's Standard, which was all very nice, but the comment I liked best was a remark from a neighbour who had worked hard all his life and done well for himself without losing his Bethnal Green accent.

"Here Val, I sent my little typist out for a Standard yesterday afternoon and the others in the office all gathered around. When they saw the address they asked if I knew you? Know her, I thought - I was the love of her life and here she is having it off with Lester Piggott and Willie Carson."

CHAPTER SEVEN

On the Tuesday Simon contacted me to say that Music Adored needed a race and he had entered her for a two-and-half mile chase at Lingfield the following Saturday. The boys and girls booked their coach and some of my enthusiasm must have rubbed off on Steve, who was not a racing man. He decided to come along to see what it was all about.

Fortunately the rain held off and racing was on at Lingfield on the Saturday – it's a course that easily becomes waterlogged with heavy rain. Steve wanted to take his car and stop for lunch. I would have liked to have gone in the coach, but he had been so good I thought it best to fall in with his wishes, so I phoned Jim at the Blacksmith's Head at Newchapel, about a mile down the road from the racecourse. It was a favourite with racegoers as the food is always good and exciting and everyone receives a warm welcome from Jim and Joan.

As usual, their timing was perfect. Jim had seen to it that lunch was prepared early to enable everyone to get to the course in plenty of time for the first race.

The scene in the parade ring was truly colourful, with the springy bright green turf, the lovely trees and flowers and the ladies all togged up for the day in case they were caught by the television cameras. It all blended in beautifully with the jockeys in their bright and jazzy colours.

Amanda Neale-Adamson was giving her jockey a leg-up on Ongar, one of her father's horses, which was being ridden that day by Lord

Hatherley-Jones. He normally only rode his own horses, but had agreed to ride Ongar for Amanda as the jockey had taken a nasty fall in the previous race and the doctor would not pass him fit to ride.

His lordship was popular with the racing public and bookies alike for his courage and good nature, and just for being a good sport. He must have broken every bone in his body at some time or other, but he kept going, and even rode in a couple of Nationals. He was very tall and thin with a pale complexion, and as the stable colours were predominantly white, they emphasised the paleness even more.

"Blimey, guv!" some joker in the crowd shouted. "You look like a bleedin' bottle of milk!'

Music Adored ran a good race, which she needed, and came in third. Ongar was coming up to the post last of the seven and Hatherley-Jones was getting a terrific cheer from the crowds, just for managing not to part company, but it was becoming increasingly obvious with every stride that Ongar was not going to make it to the post.

His jockey pulled him up and was about to dismount when Ongar just bowled right over, taking his rider with him. Hatherley-Jones hit the rails, gashing his cheek badly. The horse was still down as the jockey got to his feet and propped himself up against the rails of the grandstand.

The vet ordered the screens to be brought, and depression settled temporarily over the crowd. It is always a sad and gloomy atmosphere when a horse has to be put down.

I had known the Hon. Amanda Neale-Adamson, owner, trainer and breeder, when Ken had his horses at her yard. She had married Stuart Neale-Adamson, a very ambitious businessman, at nineteen. They appeared totally unsuitable to each other. Amanda's heart was obviously with her horses; she was a good trainer and did her job well. It was generally thought that Stuart had married her because her father, Lord Franklinford, a nutty do-gooder, had all the right connections. He was commonly known as St Paul. The more murders someone had committed, the harder he fought to get them released from jail. I had heard in racing circles that he'd been glad when Stuart proposed, as with Amanda's lack of femininity he was unable to visualize young men lining up for the privilege.

They lived on a fine estate near Newmarket. The Canadians had taken it over for their officers to use during the Second World War and restored it to its original beauty when they left, adding all the latest mod cons. When I had gone there with Ken once, I'd been very impressed by the layout. There was a long circular drive, up to the house, boarded by trees and flower beds, which surrounded the lawns they sometimes used as bowling greens. There were sunken gardens, tennis courts, a swimming pool and a lake - and then we had reached the really impressive part, the stables. They were really something. It looked as though there was everything there an owner could possibly wish for, but something must have been lacking for Ken not to have wanted to keep his horses there.

I walked over to offer my condolences to Amanda, and she cut me dead. I knew how she was feeling, particularly as this was the second horse to die on her within a few weeks. I had been getting the cold shoulder from her since Ken had taken his horses away from her yard.

I had no idea why Ken had made that sudden decision to put his horses with Simon Galloway, but knowing Ken there had to be a good reason, and certainly it would have been a decision he must have given much thought to. He was not impulsive by nature.

Poor Amanda, it was impossible for her to disguise her feelings. I saw her pacing up and down outside the changing rooms, waiting for Hatherley-Jones to reappear. He had had to see the doctor to give him the once-over and put a dressing on his face, and he had then gone in to change into his outdoor clothes.

He was hardly out of the door when Amanda pounced on him,

but I doubted if there was anything he could tell her to put her out of her misery. Only the vet would be able to come up with the answer.

Ongar must have been a disappointment to her all the way along the line. It was unlikely that he would have ever hit the headlines if he had not dropped down dead in front of Tats. One day a good jockey might have been able to get him first past the post, but in all probability the best part of the field would have had to have fallen for him to accomplish it.

Perhaps it would have been better if I hadn't approached her. It must have been doubly agonising for her to see Music Adored run such a good race, particularly as she had bred her. She obviously didn't want to lose any of Ken's horses to Simon, but it must have been extremely painful to see Music Adored go, particularly as everyone seemed to think she was going to turn out to be an exceptionally good horse.

In the meantime, St Paul was wallowing in all the sympathy he was getting from his old cronies, who were patting him on the shoulder and muttering a few inaudible words. Amanda looked livid - it was she who loved the horses. The old man would not even have known which of his horses had died if its name hadn't been over its box at the yard.

"Well, Val, this is it, your first time in the unsaddling enclosure as an owner. How's it feel?"

"Wonderful!"

"Let's hope it's the first of many."

And what a thrill it was. True, it was only third place, but Simon was more than pleased with Music's performance and her precious blanket was being given its first airing. The boys and girls bad been warned not to put their money on her to win, and at the same time Simon happened to mention that another horse, jointly owned with his brother and being ridden by him, was fit and, barring accidents, was in with a chance. It obliged, and the gang showed a profit on the day. They were as excited as I was, and I would have loved to have shared their joy on the coach home.

There is nothing like the relaxing stroll back to the coach together, exchanging all the little tit-bits of the afternoon. You felt tired, but it was a nice tiredness, especially if you had come out on the right side. Then there was the fun of unpacking all the eats and drinks that always tasted so much nicer when eaten picnic fashion.

Philip Hunt, St Paul's secretary and a first euphonist in the band, was making his way across the owners' and trainers' car park when I spotted him.

I managed to catch up with him.

"Philip, please tell Lord Franklinford how sorry I am about Ongar. Oh, and by the way, I was hoping I would see you today. Earlier this week I was turning out a cupboard at the office where Ken kept his personal papers, and I found a file with letters and cuttings about the band. I think the band secretary should have them. If I drop them into you, would you hand them over on practice night for me please?"

He seemed miles away; in fact I was not sure if he was taking in what I was saying, but then something clicked.

"Yes, of course. In I'll be passing your house tonight at about eight-thirty to nine. If you like I can pick them up then."

"Fine, I'll see you then."

Steve had enjoyed his day – in fact he was getting the fever. He said he would like to go again.

"Val, do you mind if we made it a quick meal on the way home, I have a lot of work to catch up with?"

"If you'd rather Steve. I can make myself something when I get home if you prefer, and I am rather tired after all the excitement."

He looked as though he was quite pleased with my suggestion.

"I'll tell you what, I'll give you a ring early in the week, and we will make up for it with a slap-up dinner one evening, how's that?"

"Great, I'll look forward to it." He just couldn't wait to spend his winnings. Beginner's luck. He would learn after a few more trips to the races.

After I'd made myself a snack I tried to settle down to read, but I was too excited. Excited, and puzzled. Puzzled that two of Amanda's horses should die so suddenly.

I turned it over in my mind. Could there be any connection? Of course, it is possible for two horses from the same stable to die in similar circumstances, but it is most unusual. I had always known that Ken could shut up like a clam if he wanted to, and when I tried to pump him about taking his horses away from Amanda he just said Simon was an up-and-coming young man who would do well in his career. But I was strongly suspicious that there was very much more to it than that. Ken was not the type to rush at things. He must have considered the move very seriously.

Philip pressed the doorbell at eight-forty-five – I could tell it had rung from the lights. My flasher unit has the reverse effect at night - instead of flashing, the lights dim. I put down my book, puffed up the cushions and went to open the front door.

It was hard to believe that a person's appearance could change so dramatically in such a short space of time. Philip looked terrible - absolutely washed out and haggard.

"Are you OK, Phil? Have you got time for a coffee?"

"Thanks Val, I could do with one."

I had noticed that he had not been his usual happy-go-lucky self for some time. In fact I had suspected that he was having an affair with Amanda, and just thought that as her father employed him he was concerned about his job.

"How about a drop of brandy in that coffee, I'm having one?"

"That would be lovely. It's been a tiring day," said Philip.

I let him take his time, and allowed the warmth of the room, the coffee and brandy to relax him a little.

"Any news about Ongar?" I ventured.

"Not yet, there'll have to be a post mortem. Amanda's feeling pretty cut up about it."

"I can imagine."

"One way or another, it's been a pretty lousy day for me too."

He held his head in his hands, and I could see he was near breaking point. "Is there anything I can do? Sometimes it helps to share a worry."

Now his hands were shaking.

"I've been such a bloody fool, and now Amanda's putting the pressure on. I just don't know which way to turn. Whatever I do I'm going to be in trouble it seems."

I was amazed at this outburst, it was so unlike Philip.

"Philip, have you stopped to eat anything today?"

"I had a sandwich at lunchtime."

"Let me make you something. What about a Spanish omelette and some French bread?"

"Sounds lovely, but I don't want to put you to any trouble."

"Won't take a minute or so."

My conscience was beginning to prick. My idea about offering him food was to get him into a mellow mood and talking, so that maybe I would learn something about the horses in Amanda's care. I soon put the omelette together and left him to enjoy it while I went to make some fresh coffee.

He looked a little more relaxed when I returned, and I was kicking ideas around in my head as to how I could pump him without it looking too obvious. Finally I decided it was better to break the ice with something a bit nearer home ground.

"How did you come to join the band, Philip?"

"It goes back a long way. When I was a kid of about eight, Mum and Dad talked me into joining the Salvation Army Band, as they wanted to get me out of the way on Sunday mornings. I started on the cornet, and worked my way up to flugelhorn, then baritone, and finished upon on the euphonium. You know, I can remember when I was about fourteen, saying to the bandleader "I'm a man now, I'm not going to play with kids any more" and walking out. But I loved the brass-band world too much. After a few weeks of not playing, I applied to the local band for a position."

I could see the tension was beginning to ebb away, so I stayed with the same theme.

"What about your first solo?"

For the first time that evening, a smile broke across Philip's face.

"A slow, tuneful melody - Watching The Wheat. It was a good job it was the wheat they were watching and not my legs, they were like jelly. It's a different story today. You have to have nerves of steel, double tonguing, triple tonguing and control of the four valves. Hardly nerves of steel now. In fact today I feel a complete wreck."

I hadn't meant to say the wrong thing, but I must have trod on a nerve. His hands went up to cover his face, and he was swaying to and fro.

"Oh Valerie, I've made such a mess of my life! What am I going to do?"

I was getting a bit hot and bothered. I hadn't anticipated this after the coffee and omelette.

"You've had a tiring and upsetting day, that's all Philip. Things will look different in the morning."

"They won't, you know. I had enough on my plate before, but now Amanda's putting the pressure on." I let him go on. "You've probably already guessed about Amanda and me. I didn't really feel too badly about it as far as Stuart was concerned. They were never suited to each other. He only married Amanda because he thought St Paul knew all the right people, and it would help him climb to the top, which no doubt it did. He's away the best part of the time. As you know, you can always find a pretty girl if you have the money, and he has. No doubt variety is the spice of life as far as he's concerned, but what I didn't reckon on, was becoming as fond of Amanda as I have. I know she looks a bit of a Plain Jane, and when she gave me the big come-on when St Paul first introduced us, I thought it was a bit of a joke. But once you get to know her she really is a very nice person. Somehow, I don't know why, we just clicked. Now I feel I don't want to let her down."

"I'm sure you won't."

I poured more coffee, without brandy this time as he was driving. Now he seemed lost for words.

"Unfortunately, it's not as easy as that. Look, if it's not boring you too much, can I tell you something about it? I feel I've got such a lot bottled up."

Boring me? I was agog.

"Go ahead, Phil, if you think it will do any good. You know I won't repeat anything."

"I can't really tell you all that is worrying me, but on top of everything else, one day last week Stuart must have decided not to go to town early as he normally does. Amanda thought he had already left, but he must have been in his study making some phone calls.

"As you know he has done very well for himself, and I have to give him his due, he's worked hard for it, but he's got this thing about getting a knighthood. It's almost become an obsession with him. Stuart's no fool, he knows better than most that the best way to go about it is to get involved in all the big charity stuff. So for a kick-off he has offered the use of the house and grounds for a fashion show, to be given by one of the big houses – it's going to be on telly. Anyway, he suddenly got it into his head to phone over to the stables to remind Amanda to get herself a dress for the special night.

"Apparently, it came out afterwards that he had been ringing for some time without getting a reply. The lads had taken the horses out for exercise, and Stuart thought that the stables must have been left without anyone in charge. He doesn't often make an appearance there, though he would be only too glad to catch someone out if this very strict rule was broken. Too much expensive gear about to be left unattended.

"Anyway, to cut a long story short, he stumbled on me and Amanda having a romp in the hay, so to speak, and to put it mildly he was not very pleased. In fact he was extremely angry. He called Amanda a silly, stupid cow. He didn't seem to be personally offended, he appeared to be more worried that it could have caused a scandal and that it would have made him lose face with his business associates.

"Honestly, Val, I thought for a moment he was going to kill her, but I suppose he hasn't got to where he is today without learning how to control himself. He finally calmed down. But he couldn't just let it stop there, he went on and on really insulting Amanda, saying how ugly she was, and that he was going to make sure to hide her behind a pillar on the night of the fashion show as it would never do for a roving camera to pick her up. Then he added that if the smell was anything like it normally was when she returned from the stables, they would rove the other way. He couldn't have been more insulting. There was no need for that, he has not exactly been a saint himself."

I refilled his cup with coffee. "How about another small brandy?"

I could run him home if necessary, he didn't live far away. I guessed that the incident he had described had not been the only reason for the state he was in. He took a sip.

"I do feel better for getting some of it off my chest. Well, now that I've started I may as well tell you what's happened today. I hope you don't mind."

Not mind? I couldn't wait.

"Well, I know Amanda was very upset about Ongar, and I'm trying to make allowances for that, but she has now come up with some scatterbrained idea about leaving Stuart and starting up elsewhere. She wants

me to go with her. You can imagine how St Paul is going to take that. I'll be for the chop, that's for sure."

He hesitated.

"You see, I know I shouldn't really be saying this to anyone, but we've known each other for a long time. I know you wouldn't repeat it, but Amanda seems to think Stuart is taking revenge by killing her horses, and trying to ruin her reputation.

"Of course I've told her I'm sure it's not true. I really do believe he feels quite proud when Amanda gets good write-ups in the press, but one or two strange things have happened at her yard recently. I know it's nothing to do with Stuart, but I can't convince her of that."

His words shook me to the core. I couldn't believe I was going to hear something so relevant to my investigation without even having to probe for it. I switched my hearing aids to their highest level. I didn't want to miss a word.

"It all started a few months ago. First Daffodil died, as you know, then the office at the yard was turned over, and then the tack room, all within a week.

"You remember Mr Stimpson, Paul's friend? He wanted his horse Ongar II to race at Auteuil. It had been entered against Amanda's wishes, because she didn't think he was ready for the race. Then a week before it was due to go it punctured its foot and the blacksmith had to put on a protective pad.

"You see, when a horse punctures or injures its foot the blacksmith has to clean it out, apply Stockholm tar, pack it out with cotton wool and put on a protective leather pad before he can put the shoe on.

So Amanda strongly advised Stimpson that they should withdraw. But he's the owner and has the last word, and he wasn't having any of that. He insisted that the horse should be sent to France.

"Tom, the head travelling lad, was keen to go, as he has a little filly of his own over there, and Paul said he would go along for the ride. Amanda said that as shoeing was a very expensive business it would be as well to race in heavy plates, as the light aluminium ones they fit for racing were unsuitable for road work. Horses need road work to get used to people and noise, so the heavy plates have to be put on again when the race is over.

"I've known her to race in heavy plates before. A lot of trainers do it if they enter a horse just to gain experience, or if it's in need of a race, but old Stimpson wouldn't allow it. He said it would ruin the horse's chances and that the light plates would have to be put on for the race.

"Anyway, the most extraordinary thing happened the following Monday when they had all returned from France. Ongar shed his plate, the one with the leather pad, and after saying a few words about French blacksmiths, Amanda phoned her own farrier to put another plate on. She had a look at the injured foot, and decided that it was no longer necessary to have the leather pad put back. She slipped it into the pocket of her old gilet.

"Then one morning a few days after that, she found someone had been turning the office over. I know she doesn't always look like a fashion plate herself, but she does keep her office and stables in order. She noticed that a couple of the drawers weren't quite shut, and that some of the papers were out of place. She doesn't keep anything too important there, she puts most of it in a strongbox at the bank in case of fire, so she wasn't particularly worried. She did have the locks changed, though.

"Later in the day Tom told her the tack room had been turned upside down, which seemed ridiculous. Then a few days later she put her hand in her pocket for a tissue, and came across the leather pad. When she pulled out the cotton wool she realised it felt heavier than it should have, so she tore it to pieces, really just to see what French blacksmiths put in their padding. Believe it or not there was a very neat little package inside it. And inside the package – fine white powder. Heroin! It must have been worth a pretty penny, street value.

"When you think about it, horses are the only animals allowed free passage in and out of the country, no quarantine for rabies or foot and mouth if all is well, and Ongar II was a big nine-year old with a very deep well to his foot to house the extra goods.

"I think the best thing she could have done would have been to have come out in the open about it, but no way could I persuade her. She insisted on keeping it and saying nothing about it. She says she could have very easily thrown the padding away without knowing what was inside. It was only sheer luck that she was so inquisitive.

"Anyway, that's her story and she's sticking to it. I've tried to warn her what a dangerous situation she was getting into. She was staking everything, but she wouldn't listen to advice. I told her, it's just not worth it Amanda, it could ruin your whole future. And you know as well as I do that she is a good trainer."

I was staggered. This was the last thing I had suspected. I had to agree with Philip about Stuart.

"I really can't see what Stuart would gain by damaging Amanda, it doesn't make sense to me." I said.

Philip was quite animated. "Of course not, it's a ludicrous idea." He got up from his chair and I noticed he was much more relaxed.

"Well Val, I must be on my way." He was dithering. "Look - I feel I have been a bit disloyal to Amanda, spilling the beans like this, but it's really because I am so worried about her. You wouldn't mention anything, would you?"

"Of course not, you know me better than that Philip. We'll forget you even called here tonight, OK?"

"Thanks for the coffee and the omelette, I feel much better now" he said. But he didn't look it.

It would have taken more than what he had told me to reduce him to the nervous wreck he had made of himself. I wondered if he knew more about the package than he was letting on.

"Would you like me to run you home?" I asked. I was a bit worried about the brandies, but I thought he would be under the limit as long as he had had no previous drinks.

"No thanks, I'm OK." I saw him to the door.

"Goodnight Philip, take care" I said.

"Don't worry, I'll be OK. And thanks, Val."

CHAPTER EIGHT

I had some cash to collect from three horses coming up out of a Yankee I had put on a couple of days previously. They were all favourites, so there was no mad rush to the bookie's office, but as I had managed to catch an earlier train than usual home from work I thought it a good opportunity to collect, and at the same time get a price on a horse I fancied for the King George on Boxing Day.

George, a horn player in the band, was behind the counter. His face was as long as one his horses. The rest of the staff looked pretty gloomy as well.

"What's up George?" I asked him. "It's full of gloom and doom in here, have the bookies been taking a beating today?"

"Worse than that, Valerie, there's been a knockout. Came up at four-to-one. Johnny and the lads are down at the Duke's Head drowning their sorrows." A knockout is what they call it when the odds are manipulated to enable backers of the favourite to get longer odds – bad news for the bookies.

"Do you think he would mind if I butted in? I wanted to ask him about an ante-post bet."

"'Course not, he'd be pleased to see you."

Johnny was very tall and handsome, six foot six with a mass of black curly hair. In the summer he wore silk monogrammed shirts unbuttoned almost to the waist and three gold chains around his neck, one bearing a gold racehorse. He always looked to me as though he would be more at home doing a James Bond scene on a film set than shouting the odds on a bookmaker's stand. I'd seen ladies at classy meetings such as Royal Ascot stagger up to Johnny's stand in their high heels, flutter their false eyelashes and have a pony (£500) each way on an old rag (outsider). Just what Johnny liked, and he knew exactly how to play up to them. He would have been quite happy if another jolly (a favourite) never passed the post.

I spotted him standing at the bar as I entered. Charlie, who was a natural at accents, was coming over with one of his endless supply of tales.

"So this Irishman said to the Father, it's a terrible thing Father, I can't stop gambling. Every day I have to go into a betting shop and put money on a horse."

"That's bad my son, bad" said the Father. "You must light a candle and say three Hail Marys every day for the next six days."

Back went Paddy on the seventh day. "Father, every day I light a candle and say three Hail Marys, but I'm still backing losers."

"This is very strange my son, which candles did you light?" "The small ones Father, I'm a bit short after losing all that money." "Ah, that's the trouble then my son, the small ones are for the dogs."

* * * * * * * * * *

The Goodwood of greyhound racing – that's what Walthamstow Stadium has always been called, and it is so true. Greyhound racing at its most luxurious. Every possible comfort that could be provided for the racegoer is there. The thickly-carpeted spacious lounges with an all-round view of the track and the soft leather seats, such a joy to sink into. The menu and service in the dining areas are comparable with tip-top hotels, often better.

The track itself is very attractive, with illuminated coloured fountains and flower-beds and an outsize clock saying how many minutes' betting time is left before the start of the next race. At the northern end of the track is a register of all the bets being placed at the windows, inclusive of all the forecast combinations, which are such a popular bet at the dogs. At the southern end, another illuminated board gives the up-to-the-minute odds.

However Johnny, George, Charlie and Bill were not there to enjoy such exquisite surroundings. They were on the outside making their books, and working very hard at it too.

For over fifty years the Chandlers of 'The Stow' as it is popularly called, have been renowned for their charity nights. They have never been known to turn down a worthwhile cause. Regularly every November the Mayor and his staff could be seen going round with their buckets, making a collection for Christmas parcels for the senior citizens of the locality. This night was no exception.

The Waltham Forest Band were there playing carols, not in their normal smart blue and black uniforms but dressed in Edwardian style to fit the occasion. The true Christmas spirit was rapidly descending upon the racegoers. The lively rhythm of Sleighride, coming over to George, made him wish he was on the other side of the fence with the band, concentrating on getting his notes right on his trombone, rather than getting his figures right on the book. However the money was coming for the first race, and they were beginning to get busy.

It was hectic, but after each race Johnny would relax a little, light a cigarette, and take things easy for a few moments while George paid out the winners of the previous race. It was during one of these relaxing moments that Johnny noticed a familiar pair of legs. One of the good things about Johnny was his memory. He could remember a shapely pair of legs as clearly as he could remember the winner of the three o'clock at Newcastle three weeks previously. The pair trotting along now to ask him for a contribution belonged to a little bird who had come into his shop and put a hundred quid on Rose

Petal the Third the day of the knockout.

Normally, he would mumble under his breath 'On the bloody ear-ole again' and tell George to put a pound in the bucket, but tonight he wanted to make an impression.

"George, a fiver for the lady! You're doing a very good job, me dear." George, unable to believe that Johnny was throwing his money around like a man with no arms, was agape, but Johnny was never slow at the start. He was remembering that the directors always entertained the Mayor and his staff to dinner in the Goodwood Lounge, and that he would have to make it up there a bit sharpish after the last race to chat her up and get some information. This was the first real lead that they had come across that was remotely connected with the knockout, and not a bad lead at that.

It was going to be a pleasure chatting her up. This, he thought, must be his lucky night, specially as most of the outsiders were romping home as well. He threw his cigarette away and started to get into his stride for the rush of last-minute bets on the next race.

As the minutes crept round on the big clock the betting really began to hot up, and for the two to three minutes before the 'off' Johnny was really going to town, grabbing the money from the punters, handing out the tickets, rubbing out and altering the prices on the board with Charlie tic-tacking over to the silver stand on the other side of the track. He was going at such speed that he would have put any self-respecting three-card trickster to shame.

After the last race Johnny rushed up the stairs to where the official party were preparing themselves to take their leave, so he would lose no time in placing himself in the right position to make contact with the young lady concerned, and he was never at a loss for words. He started to lay on the charm, but much to his dismay, for once, it didn't work.

This was a situation he had never come across before. Normally the birds chased him, so this put a big dent in his ego. However, it didn't take him long to discover the reason for her coolness. She had a young man with her, and from where Johnny was standing it looked like he knew how to handle himself.

Oh well, you can't win 'em all, he thought. At least he knew where she worked, at the Town Hall, and that she was local. They would all have to keep their eyes and ears open in future. Not that anything could be done officially. It was not a crime to beat the hook, only in the bookmakers' language, and if they could get any information as to how it was set up they would have more chance of knowing how to hedge it in future.

The professional backers, the ones with the big money, were not normally involved in a knockout. They relied on their own skill and judgment; it was their living. The knockouts usually came about when somebody got hold of a good bit of inside information, usually when a horse was fit and in tip-top condition to race, and had the money to do something about it.

The bookies had yet to tumble how the knockout was done. There are various ways, but in this particular instance the 'market racket' had been worked. I'd better explain. As everyone knows, there are wholesale fish and vegetable markets in every principal town in the country, and they all make an early start to the day and finish work around noon. About fifteen to twenty 'leaders' are selected who work in the markets and who can, to a certain extent, be trusted, in towns all over the country - Manchester, Liverpool, London, Newcastle, Birmingham and so on.

Either £1000, £2000 or £5000 is made available to each leader at very short notice before the race. They in turn each select ten men who are working in the market and who live in highly-populated areas where there are at least ten betting shops within easy reach of each other. The men must know how to get from one shop to the next pronto, and even more important, how to keep their mouths shut.

The main men at the markets are contacted approximately an hour before the race and given the name of the horse to back. They divide the money they have been given between the ten men they have selected to back the horse in ten individual bets at their ten selected shops at the latest possible moment before the "off".

Now with twenty markets placing a possible £1000, £2000, £5000 or even £10000 each around the country, that is a possible £200,000 going on in £100 bets without giving the bookmakers time to realise what is happening so they can hedge the bets and bring down the price.

The boys placing the bets are usually given £10 each to put on for themselves, to keep them sweet for the next fix, so that if the horse comes up with an SP of 4-11 they come away with £50 for ten minutes' work. They also normally put another fiver on for the missus. The technology used today is so sophisticated that other methods are having to be worked out.

However, all was not lost. On the Thursday it was Charity Night at the local Room at the Top. Many local businesses were giving their support and some well-known artists were giving their services free. It was in aid of the children's fund, and a few members of the band who were there to play the introductions had persuaded me to go along.

I had bought a £15 ticket, but thought I would feel a bit out of place on my own. However I could hardly refuse when they said they were planning to ask me to accept the Vice Presidency, which had been unfilled since the death of Ken. They appreciated that I always turned up at the functions they played at and cheered them on at the various contests they entered. It would be a fitting tribute to Ken to follow him into the job, though he would of course be a hard act to follow.

Johnny was looking more handsome than ever in his evening attire. The local betting shop was making a generous contribution to the evening.

It was a pity that nobody had thought to ask Charlie to partake in the entertainment. He could have kept them amused for hours with his string of tales. He was where he could usually be found at the bar, with a crowd round him, as usual, all waiting for the latest. Off went Charlie with another story.

"So this rabbi said to his assistant, 'now go down to the Catholic Church and see why they do more business than we do'. Off went Ivor, and was back within half an hour.

"Ivor, vy are you back so soon?'

"Because I know vy zey are so busy. No sooner are they in there than a geezer comes round with a plate to collect the bets."

He called the barman over for a refill.

"Anyway this rabbi was even more annoyed when the priest, who lived opposite him, went out and bought a new Mini, brought it home and baptised it by sprinkling holy water on the bonnet. Off rushed the Rabbi. He came back with a Jag and chopped a couple of inches off the exhaust."

I'm sure Charlie could have kept it up all night, but it was time for us to take our seats for the dinner. Johnny could not believe his eyes when he saw he was going to be sitting opposite the girl with the smashing legs, and minus the boyfriend. Instead she was being escorted by her old man, who owned a shop in the High Street.

It didn't take Johnny long, once the dinner and speeches were over, to become more closely acquainted with her. He knew how to put on the charm, and at the same time he managed to bamboozle her with talk about winners and prices and to ask her opinion about various performances.

She was completely flummoxed. "I'm sorry, I don't know anything at all about horses and racing" she said. "I've never been to a racecourse in my life before."

Johnny was really laying it on thick. "Oh come on, you don't expect me to believe that do you? I remember when you came into my shop and put a ton on a horse that won easily at 4-11. You have to know about racing to come up with something like that."

She was most indignant. "That wasn't for me, it was for my boyfriend. I only ever have 50p on the Derby and Grand National."

"If you'll pardon me saying so, your boyfriend must have a very good job to be able to put that sort of money on a horse" Johnny went on.

Now she was really pouting. "My Brian wouldn't put a pound on a horse, let alone £100."

This Johnny could well believe. From what he had seen of Brian he looked a right skinflint, not at all the type to contribute to the expensive upkeep of a bookmaker's life-style.

"We're saving up to get married. Brian wouldn't throw his money away like that. He put it on for a friend where he works at the fish market. He agreed to put ten bets on for him, but Brian's car was playing up that day and he was afraid he wouldn't be able to get to all the shops in time. I had a day's leave and we were going to look at some furniture that afternoon, so I said I would help him. Did it win?"

I glanced over at Johnny. I could imagine what was going through his mind. Oh cor blimey, did it win!

It makes your heart bleed, but at least he now knew how the trick was being set up. The next thing would be to find out who was behind it. It had to be someone who could afford it and was copping hold of some good information, as well as having connections in the markets. Not much to go on, but should narrow the field down a bit.

Johnny made a mental note to send a memo to his other shops to keep an eye open for last-minute betting in tons, and to hedge straight away while there was still time. Once this sort of thing started it was inclined to roll.

Some of the bookies decided to get their own back by keeping the prices down at the afternoon dogs to about 2-11 at the track, hedging a load of bets, and then putting up the prices to around 7-11 just before the off to get a good return price on their hedge bets.

As I opened the front door, I could see the light flashing on the telephone in the hall. I just managed to get to it as Steve was about to hang up.

"Hello Val, had a good evening?"

"Super, and they raised about £12,000 on the night."

"Good show. I wondered if you'd seen tonight's paper. Another horse has died, in rather similar circumstances. Not one of Amanda's this time. There seem to have been a few horses dying in the same way over the past year. I thought you might like to check, see if they happened to be insured by the same person. At the same time you might see if anything else connects. I noticed myself that the last three horses to die have all been past their prime and towards the end of their racing career. May just be a coincidence, of course. We'll have to get together on this Val, two heads have got to be better than one. Give me a ring tomorrow and let me know if you come up with anything. Goodnight my dear, sleep well."

I knew he meant well, but I was at a loss to understand how he could tell me to 'sleep well' after filling my head with so many questions. Surely I would be all night trying to figure out the answers. But I had nothing to worry about. As soon as my head hit the pillow, I was asleep.

CHAPTER NINE

On my way to church the following Sunday, I made up my mind to have another word with Our Lady and ask her help to untangle the mystery of Ken's accident – or, as I had come to believe, his murder. I was determined to get to the bottom of it. I would never ever accept the coroner's verdict.

The church was as beautiful as ever and the priest looked superb in his new vestments, but there was a problem - everyone was looking very glum. There had been gale during the week and the roof needed some immediate repair if further damage to the church was to be avoided. Everyone was thinking up ways to raise some money, quite a lot of it and quickly.

So it was back to the dog track. I had got to know Percy, the boss, through the various charities I had supported there, so I went to see him and begged him to let the choir do some Christmas carols and songs to raise some money for the roof.

I could see what he was thinking - dog racing and church choirs do not mix. But I explained that we would dress up in Christmassy gear and bring our gold outside candles, which are very decorative. We would keep to well-known Christmas songs and carols, such as White Christmas and Rudolf the Red-Nosed Reindeer.

He was not really convinced, but after thinking it over he said they always had a free night just before Christmas - no entrance fee - and he thought that some people might decide to give, as they did not have to pay to go in.

He suggested we stand behind the turnstiles at the main entrance and hope for the best.

The lads and lasses of the choir did not have time to rig up Christmas gear, so they took along with them cassocks, mitres, choir robes and anything else they could think of to make a bit of a show. Percy came down before racing began to see how we were getting on. He was gobsmacked to see the money pouring into the buckets. Not only that but many people were standing actually listening instead of rushing through to get their money on the first race.

He seemed genuinely surprised that the choir was so good. There and then he asked me to ask them if they would stay after racing and sing some popular songs in the Goodwood lounge.

"I'm sure they would love to, Percy, but they have all come here straight from work and haven't eaten," he said.

"No problem, I'll arrange for food and drinks for them on the house."

"What, all twenty-four of them?"

"Of course. And we'll make a donation."

He arranged for the money we had collected to be taken to the strong room along with our golden candles. I was amazed to see a fantastic machine there which sorts the money out - you just pour it all in. The staff in there did this for us and it was all sorted within a matter of minutes. Then they exchanged it for notes, which made the going home so much easier and safer.

I had only taken a fiver with me, as I didn't want to be lumbered with a handbag, and as the boys and girls said they had no money I put the note in the centre of the table and suggested we took it in turns to select a dog and put fifty pence on, so that we had an interest for the eight races.

Just before the seventh race Percy leaned over and whispered in my ear. "If your friends fancied a bet I think the number four dog should do quite well," he said.

Miraculously they all managed to find five and ten pound notes, which they hadn't had before, and of course the number four dog walked home.

The following week I was reading the local paper, as I had taken an interest in it since the phony reporter had turned up at Simon's yard. What a giggle I had when I saw the headline on the Sports Page: CLERGY LINE UP FOR THEIR WINNINGS AT WALTHAMSTOW.

* * * * * * * * *

My neighbour Sonia was the biggest snob I have ever known – a friend of Lady Tuckington, Lady This, Lady That. She thought she was slumming it having to live next door to me, poor soul, and a polite good morning or good evening was all that was ever exchanged between us.

One day Sonia's husband, a very well-groomed man who regularly had his hair permed, was having morning coffee and a pastry when he keeled over with a heart attack. He was dead before he hit the floor. Her ladyship found the key to the liquor cupboard, and it was all downhill from then on.

When she finally ran out of booze she opened the door to a gentleman who had been trying for a week to get an answer. The lady who had always looked so ravishing at Ascot or Henley with her husband now looked like something out of a Frankenstein film. She had not taken her negligé off for a week. Her hair, which was normally in a bun, had come adrift and was hanging loose over her face, which at least had the benefit of hiding what was underneath.

The visitor, a friend of her late husband, had promised to look after Sonia after his demise. He had arranged the funeral, and the hearse was on its way. They finally levered her out of the house and sat her in the car to follow the hearse.

A few days after the funeral this gentleman called on me and asked if I would keep an eye on his late friend's widow. I told him I worked full time and did not want the responsibility. He was not put off. He asked me if I would get her some food if he gave me fifty pounds. He was also leaving a cheque book for her to pay the electricity, gas, rates and so on.

She had never had a cheque book before, because although her husband opened accounts for her to buy clothes and she did have beautiful things, he would never give her cash. That was understandable. However she managed to find a little corner shop run by an Asian family, and persuaded them to let her have whatever drink she wanted in return for a cheque.

I had been told there was no shortage of money, so I was very surprised one day when Sonia asked me to lend her a teabag. It seems she had begun to do this on a regular basis, knocking on all the doors to ask for a teabag or a slice of bread. I asked her why she couldn't buy the tea and bread herself.

"I haven't got any money," she said.

"I thought you had plenty of money?"

"No" she said. "The cheques have all run out."

It was listening for Sonia's knocks and rings at the door that made me realise my hearing was getting really bad. It wasn't long after this that someone suggested I should apply for a hearing dog for deaf people. I was a little unsure about this, as I did not want to be too restricted, but I was assured that hearing dogs were welcome in most places, so before I made up my mind I decided to write to all my favourite racecourses to ask if I would be able to take my dog.

The racecourses all said that a hearing dog would be very welcome, which gave me a terrific lift. I sent off for an application form. The first thing was an audiological test - you have to be severely deaf before you are considered. Then a placement officer visited me for an assessment, to see what my dog needed to be trained for.

A little later on I got a letter with a photograph to say that a dog had been chosen for me and would I go to the Training Centre to meet the dog -see if we were compatible, because if we weren't it would not work.

I was very excited, couldn't wait to get there, and luckily Kayla and I hit it off straight away. So now the training could begin in earnest.

CHAPTER TEN

All this rather distracted me from my quest to find out what had really happened to Ken. I kept reminding myself to examine once again the files on money paid out for horses that had died suddenly, but Christmas was coming and I thought it best to start my investigations afresh in the New Year.

I was looking forward to Kempton on Boxing Day for the King George. I'd been going there for as along as I could remember. Many years ago we used to take a hamper of turkey sandwiches and a bottle of wine and pay three shillings and sixpence to go up on the terrace and freeze for the rest of the afternoon. It's a very different story today. It costs £185 for the day at the Jubilee Club, but it's worth every penny.

I always book from one year to the next as it is so popular, and have the same table near the tote and the bar so that everything is to hand without too much disturbance. There's coffee and pastries on arrival, a fabulous lunch and tea in the afternoon and hopefully a few winners. It has a bit of a carnival atmosphere about it and everyone seems to be in a good mood, punters and staff alike.

Old Albert had made Kempton his second home. He would bring his little pack of sandwiches each day and pay the girls 35p to make him a cup of tea or coffee from time to time. He sat in his little corner every day from opening time until they closed. He was quite harmless and everyone was used to seeing him around, but he would give tips. They never came up of course, and nobody took any notice, but on this particular day he was giving anybody that would listen to him a tip for a horse that they were laying at 7-11. The race began and everyone had their eyes glued to the television screens.

As it happened, the horse got a flyer at the start and was soon five to six lengths in front, looking as though nothing was going to catch it. Then, out of the blue, it dropped dead. It had burst a blood vessel - it happens from time to time.

When old Albert saw the horse lying on the track, he keeled over as well. They all rushed to bring him round, but nothing could be done. He had died of shock.

The next day the police came into the betting shop to say they were trying to get his body identified. They had been to Albert's flat and asked his neighbours, but it seemed he had no living relatives. Would a couple of the men from the racecourse identify him?

They put their heads together and came to the conclusion that this was the least they could do by way of a last service for old Albert. Off they went to the mortuary, where a new mortician's assistant has just started that week. He took them along a corridor and into a room and pulled out the first drawer, gently lowering the sheet to reveal the deceased.

"That's not Albert," they said in harmony.

"Sorry sir, maybe I got the wrong drawer."

He pulled out the next drawer and again gently lowered the sheet.

"Nope, that's not him either."

Flustered now, the young mortician opened the third drawer.

"Sorry, that's not Albert either," said our man. "But that's typical. He never was in the first three."

* * * * * * * * *

It was a miserable day, overcast and drizzling, when I bumped into Philip at Lingfield. I hardly recognised him. He looked ten years older, his hair was turning grey, and he had lost a lot of weight.

"Hi Philip, how are you?"

"Not bad Val, not bad."

But I could see that he was lying. He was a shadow of his former self.

"Look Val, we can't talk here, but I'd like to have a word with you" he muttered. "A lot's been happening recently. With hindsight I think Ken was on to it, or at least some of it. He knew a lot of people in the racing world. It wouldn't surprise me if somebody had spoken to him about the strange events of the last year or two."

"Phil, I have been certain from day one that Ken's car crash was no accident. But what could I do? No one would believe me. There was no other vehicle involved, and once the coroner said it was accidental death I was on my own. Steve's been very good trying to help, but we haven't got very far. The police have made it quite clear they're not prepared to investigate further."

"I'd like to talk about it," said Phil. "How about coming and having a bit of dinner with me one evening when you're passing my way?"

"OK, how about tonight? I really want to get this off my chest."

"Not if you don't mind a take-away, I won't have time to cook."

"No, that's fine. I'll bring the wine."

I don't know if it was the miserable weather or the prospect of learning what Phil had to say, but I couldn't seem to concentrate on finding winners. It was a losing day. It reminded me of a bad day years ago when my family were with me. They were singing "There's a pawn shop round the corner in Pittsburgh, Pennsylvania..."

No pawn shop, but not much cash in my purse either. I'd have to resort to a credit card for the takeaway.

Kayla made herself comfortable in the car on the way home. It had been her first day's racing, and she had really enjoyed it. So many people made such a big fuss of her.

I made sure the place was warm and bright for Philip when he arrived, as he certainly needed cheering up. He hit it off with Kayla straight away, and I think he found some comfort in cuddling up to her and stroking her. Of course, she was loving it.

The Indian meal and the wine made us both more relaxed, which was just as well. I wasn't sure what I was going to hear, or how I was going to deal with it. Just as well we left it until we got to the coffee, it's very difficult to lip-read someone who's eating. Go into a restaurant or café where a deaf group is having an outing, and you'll find there is complete silence during the meal.

"It's that silly fool St Paul" Philip began. "He's got himself into trouble through his do-good visits to prisons, trying to save the hard-done-by inmates. It was a time-bomb waiting to go off. It was a racing certainty that one day the old lags would get to him, and now it's happened. He's being blackmailed. He's digging himself in deeper all the time, and dragging me into it with him. As you know, I've worked for him for years. On the whole I've been happy in the job, but these last months have been a nightmare."

"So how does it work? What are they doing?" I was fascinated.

"One of the prisoners is a member of an East End gang, and they've been running a bit of a protection racket round the market stalls. Small potatoes, just throwing ink over the clothes or tipping things over if they didn't get their weekly dosh. Well, it's coming to an end. The stallholders are getting together. They're beginning to stand up for themselves on payout day. So Chopper's gang had to think up a new get-rich-quick scheme, and St Paul gave them just what they needed.

"Chopper and his mates had decided that St Paul would do what he was told or the horses would suffer. That's what happened to Amanda's horses."

"So what have they been doing to them? The bastards!" I was angry now.

"Ragwort's been found in the hay, and acorns have been spread about where the horses graze. Both poisonous of course if they eat too much. They're now getting at him to try and bribe the stable lads and lasses, but of course they love the horses too much. They'd do anything rather than harm them."

"So what's Franklinford going to do about it?"

"You know how I've spoiled him all these years, keeping everything in apple-pie order. Now he thinks I can get this gang off his back for him, but it's not that easy. Remember when I said Amanda had found drugs in the shoe of the horse that was sent to France? That was just part of a much bigger operation."

"Do you think this has anything to do with what happened to Ken?"

"Could be. I think Ken must have known something about all this. Maybe they didn't intend to kill him, just give him a warning to make sure he kept quiet. That was never going to work. A man of Ken's integrity wasn't going to be put off."

"The question is - where do we go from here?"

We mulled it over together.

"What if I had a word with Steve and put him in the picture about what you've told me tonight?" I suggested. "He uses an agent from time to time. He even suggested some time ago that we should bring him in, but we had so little to go on. Now perhaps we've got something he could work on."

"That's a fantastic idea. But who's going to pay? I certainly can't afford all those fees and expenses."

"You don't have to. Steve and I will look after the bill. You just keep us in the picture as things develop."

I knew Steve would be willing, and felt sure the firm would agree to cover the cost if it meant Mike could unravel this growing mystery.

I met Steve the next day. He was very interested in what I had to tell him. He said he would contact Mike straight away and give him the facts to get him going. Mike came over a few minutes later.

A grin slowly spread over Mike's face when we told him. "Oh yes – Chopper. Mr Stevenson. I know the gentleman you're referring to, and his mates. As a matter of fact, without breaking any client confidentiality, I'm working on something about him at the moment."

Steve was all ears. "Can you tell us anything?"

"You probably know he's been running a protection racket, in a small way, in the East End markets for years. Every Friday he and his heavies go round to collect their donations, as they like to call them. The stallholders have always paid up to keep the peace. They comforted themselves that they only had to sell one more jacket or dress or another box of apples and pears to pay for it.

"Now it's all changing. The life of the stallholder isn't as easy as it used to be. They're having to set up stall six days a week to make a living, with all the competition from the high street. They've started digging their heels in.

There've been one or two skirmishes recently with those who have refused.

Now they've asked me for help."

"I'll get on to it straight away" said Mike. "It'll be the usual fee plus expenses. I'll send you a report as soon as I find anything out."

CHAPTER ELEVEN

It was chaos on the Central Line as usual, and I was getting uptight about getting to the City Lit in time. I was going to a meeting for people who had become deaf suddenly and were finding it difficult to cope. I had been warned some time ago that my hearing would only get worse, so I had joined a signing class to learn British Sign Language, though I preferred Sign Supported English. I was not particularly good at it, but it helped me to get by from time to time.

At the meeting they had Palanatype on a large screen, a lip-speaker and an interpreter of sign language, but even with all this I was finding it difficult to follow.

When we broke up for coffee, I got into conversation with a gentleman who introduced himself as Dr Colin Green. He was not much to look at, short, skinny and wrinkled, but he clearly had a wonderful sense of humour. He told me that he had tripped on a kerb one day when getting out of his car, knocked his head against a concrete lamp-post, and hadn't heard a thing since. The way he told it, it was the funniest thing that had ever happened.

It is very sad for professional people who lose their hearing suddenly in middle age. They have usually established themselves in a good job, with a family and a mortgage and find themselves unable to carry on with their profession. I have seen it happen to teachers in particular.

Colin Green told me he could manage quite well, thanks to a very efficient secretary who had been with him for years, and knew the routine and general running of the surgery inside out. Whenever she went on holiday, however, and he had to bring in a temp, things started to go wrong. Only the previous week there had been an embarrassing mix-up between two Mrs Hills who both happened to live in Carisbrooke Road. Old Mrs Hill had rung in to say she had had a fall and hurt her leg. The temp gave him the wrong house, and he was rather puzzled on arrival to find the door opened by the other Mrs Hill, a young and curvaceous blonde in a very short skirt. "Mrs Hill? Sounds as if I need to take a good look at your legs" he had said the minute she let him in.

The meeting was helpful in many ways, but I was beginning to wonder if I would ever adapt to this silent world.

The following Sunday the band had entered the South of England competition, and they invited me to go along with them to Brighton. We had to make an early start because the competition began at ten o'clock, and they liked to get there early to change into their uniforms and settle down.

I popped a few bottles of Bucks Fizz and some plastic wine glasses into a coolbag in case there was a need for celebration on the way home. They usually played well, and managed to capture some prize.

The competitions were held in a very large hall where a sort of open-topped tent had been erected in the centre. The band had to play inside the tent so that the judges could not see who was playing. They relied on their marking solely by the sound.

I went off to find a nice little church, as there was little point in my staying. The familiar smell of incense as I entered made me feel quite at home. It was a lovely service, all smells and bells as they like to say in the High Church, and they made me very welcome.

I strolled back to the concert hall to see how the band was getting on. They had played and were free to go to lunch. Bill and five other members had booked a lunch at a small private hotel, and they asked me to go with them.

Brighton was at its best, and the weather was being kind, quite warm and bracing. I was beginning to feel as if I was on my holidays as we walked along the prom taking in the good sea air. The men were in high spirits. They felt they had played really well that morning, so it was turning out to be a good day.

It was an old-fashioned family-run hotel, which was spotlessly clean. They offered good home cooking, and the dinner smelled delicious. They served the vegetables in small stainless steel dishes. Bill was sitting next to me. He urged me to have some courgettes. They looked liked carrots to me, a vegetable I dislike, but rather than argue with him I took some. They tasted like carrots as well. Very puzzling.

The following Tuesday I met Bill's wife. She told me that now the competition was over, they were going on holiday. Bill insisted on driving, but she was unhappy about this because he found it difficult to follow the traffic lights – he was colour blind. Now I know why he thought the carrots were courgettes.

The band finished second, and the atmosphere in the coach going home was terrific.

I wondered how Mike was getting on back on London. My fingers were firmly crossed.

CHAPTER TWELVE

Mike knew the East End like the back of his hand. He had many connections he could call on, as well as a network of snouts he could pay for information.

He started by consulting his little black book to work out who to approach about Chopper. He decided to start with Charlie at the bookies. Charlie knew about everybody, and his information went back a long way. His father had been in his prime when the Krays' reign was at its height. He had worked for them from time to time as an odd job man, running errands and doing run-of-the-mill jobs. He was not into the violent side, but he saw plenty of it just the same.

Charlie was always at the races with Johnny making a book. He was his chief clerk, and an expert at figures. He might have made a good accountant if he had had the opportunity to go to college when he was younger.

Much as he liked mixing with those on the other side of the fence, he was determined to go straight himself. He had seen too much heartache when he was young as a result of the wars between the gangs his father worked for. He loved his family and would guard them very carefully to make sure no harm came to them, but his unique position did enable him to pick up plenty of good tips, which he passed to Mike from time to time.

Charlie was propping up the bar at the Duke's Head as usual when Mike found him.

"Wotcher mate, how's it going?" said Mike.

"OK Mike, you all right? Something tells me you're gonna bend my ear. Make it a scotch, a double".

"Wanna go and sit by the window? We don't want Patsy joining in every two minutes."

Patsy was a good listener. Too good, sometimes. The men picked up their drinks and made their way towards a table in the corner.

"It's about Chopper. A couple of his oppos seem to be missing."

"Yeah, that's right. Boots." (Boots had got his name for always wearing the same winkle-picker boots since he'd been a Teddy Boy in the sixties.) "He's in the Scrubs, went down for GBH when one of their clients wouldn't cough up. Don't know much about the other one, they sent him to some jail up north.

"What about the rest?"

"Sticks has just got out. He's been laughing his head off since he got home, telling everyone that that idiot St Paul is trying to turn him into a born-again Christian. He's playing up to it, telling him he's going to turn over a new leaf. Some hopes."

What a break. Mike could see why Sticks wanted to play up to St Paul, so that he would keep visiting and Boots could put more and more pressure on him about the horses. It was such a waste of time. It was never going to go anywhere beyond the initial stages, but they really believed that he could somehow fix races. They couldn't see that St Paul just wasn't clever enough. He was just fumbling about, getting himself, Philip and Amanda in a right old state. Yet he really thought that if he supplied Philip with the necessary, Philip would bribe the stable-lads and lasses.

No chance. Philip knew that the technology was just too advanced now. There wasn't a hope in hell of putting it into practice.

In the meantime they kept on threatening to kill more horses. It was becoming increasingly obvious that the deaths hadn't just been bad luck. Their feed was being tampered with.

Mike's next move was to call on Philip. He decided to take the bull by the horns and be completely up front with him, not divulging Steve's name but saying he was working for a client who wanted to put a stop to this stupid nonsense once and for all. Val had told Steve how upset Philip was and Steve had passed the word on to Mike. He felt it was worth the trip to Newmarket to talk to St Paul's right-hand man.

He was not disappointed. Philip was beginning to reach the end of his tether and was glad of any help he could get. He was still a hundred per cent loyal to St Paul, but he had had enough of trying to make him see sense. He felt he was between the devil and the deep blue sea. He was more than willing to talk to Mike.

"St Paul knows what Boots and his mates are capable of' Philip told Mike. "He's scared of getting a beating. He'll promise to try and ward them off, but they aren't as soft as he is. Making promises he can't keep is making it worse."

Mike sent in his first report to Steve, feeling he had made good headway in a couple of days. But there was more work to be done.

* * * * * * * * * * *

That Saturday two members of the band were getting married, and it was a glorious day. The rest of the band were going to play of course, and form a guard of honour with their instruments as the couple left the church.

The women in the band had made a magnificent job of the flowers in the church. They were all blue and white, as the predominant colour of the band was blue. They had made their first visit to the New Spitalfields Market at Leyton to buy the flowers, and they had not been disappointed. There was so much to choose from, and a shop where they could buy all the accessories they needed.

It was a truly happy occasion and everybody was in good spirits. David, the best man, made an excellent speech, with some good jokes about the antics of the band. After the ceremony Philip came over to say how sad it was that Ken could not be with us on this very special day.

"He would have loved it, Val," he said. Wouldn't he just, I thought.

"I know this isn't exactly the time to ask you a favour, but I wondered if you could you have a look in Ken's private cupboard at the office, when you have a minute? He may have left some music there that he was going to bring them to the band meeting. I know you've had so much to cope with recently, so I didn't want to bother you with it till now."

"No problem, Philip, I'll make a note. I'm sure I can find time during the week to have a look. I should have done something about that cupboard before now, but there's been so much work to get through."

"By the way, I had a visit the other day. Nice young fellow called Mike. I must say I feel a lot better now that someone professional's looking into this scam. He seemed to be with it. He was very open and above board with me. He knew of St Paul's involvement, but he didn't know how far in he was."

"I'm glad you got on all right with him."

"I told him I had to be loyal to St Paul as I had worked for him for so many years and he's been so kind to me. I said I didn't want to be mixed up with anything illegal. It's been quite a burden to me over the last few months, you know."

"It's OK Philip, you mustn't worry about the call. I do know about it. He's one of Steve's agents. I felt things were getting out of hand, so I had a word with him, asked him to get someone on the case."

Some of the worry-lines on Philip's face seemed to have disappeared.

"He left me his card with his office and home number. Well, now

I know who he's working for, I'll rack my brains and let him know if I can remember anything."

"Thanks Philip. Isn't this a wonderful wedding? It's the first time I've felt really happy since last October."

A few days later I made a start on the cupboard. First I thought I would look through a few files again, to see if I could find any connection to the present situation.

It did appear rather strange that a number of horses had died in the past two years as a result of laminitis. I decided to get a book from the library and read up about it. At least it would give me something more to think about. I was still puzzled about Philip being so upset, and wondered if he knew more than he was telling me. I'd have to make sure I had another chat with him the next time the band was playing at a function.

He was such a nice man, and it couldn't be easy for him working for St Paul. He was getting more eccentric by the day, and constantly upsetting Amanda by telling her what to do with the horses, though he knew nothing whatsoever about training. Philip had told me the atmosphere at the stables was very bad and some of the staff were threatening to leave.

I hadn't got very far with the contents of the cupboard before it was time to take Kayla home. I didn't think it was fair to make her do so much overtime so early in her new job.

What fun it was travelling home together, everybody in the carriage fussing over Kayla. It made my journey home so much more friendly. Normally everybody had their heads in the evening paper.

Kayla was really beginning to prove her worth. She would let me know when a fax were coming through, and if there was a fire alarm practice she would alert me and then lie flat on the floor, to tell me it was the fire alarm. Although she was very protective, she had not been specifically trained to ward off any intruders, but I felt much better about staying in the office after the rest of the staff had gone home, knowing she'd be with me. I had not plucked up the courage to stay there alone since the night someone had been snooping in the office.

CHAPTER THIRTEEN

Steve was quite cross with me when I told him what I'd been doing.

"I told you Val, you must not stay there on your own in the evenings. It's too dangerous" he told me. At least this meant he was now taking the matter more seriously.

Mike had now been in contact with the market traders, suggesting they play Chopper and his heavies at their own game. He said he could round up quite a few bouncers from the night clubs and dance halls. The traders had a meeting and agreed to put in £50 each to pay them. If it worked, they wouldn't have to pay Chopper's boys again.

So the following Friday, when the extortioners got there as usual, they found a line of bouncers waiting for them. Mike was there, as spokesman. He told the mob that if they wanted to act rough they were ready for it. When Chopper's thugs saw the size of the ex-wrestlers and heavyweight boxers he had picked, they didn't hang around. They knew their little racket had come to an end. Time to go off and find easier pickings somewhere else

A few days later Charlie got in touch with Mike, and they agreed to meet that evening when the betting shop closed. There was a double scotch waiting for Charlie when he arrived, and he knew he would be on a few quid from Mike, who was always fair about any information received.

"There's a whisper going round that Chopper's lost his steady income and he's looking to make it up somewhere else" said Charlie.

"Well seeing as I'm the man who lost it for him, I think you need to tell me a bit more than that" said Mike.

"Well, you know he and his mob sell drugs to the kids on the streets and at the rave-ups? They're saying there's not enough in it for them. They are really only acting as distributors. They want to get hold of the stuff as it comes into the country and buy direct. Cut out the middleman, so to speak. Sparks reckons he knows who's supplying the transport, but he's keeping it to himself for the time being."

Mike smiled and dug out a wad of notes. He counted off a few and slipped them to Charlie.

"There's more where that came from if you can find out a few details," he said.

"I'll be in touch Mike. Always pleased to do business with you."

Charlie's information gave Mike plenty to think about, but he couldn't see what connection there might be between Chopper's drugs scheme and tampering with horses' feed. It was time to do some serious thinking.

He decided to get out his blackboard and chalk. Then he wrote down everything he had learned from the beginning.

One name was connected to everything else – Lord Franklinford. He was Amanda's father and Philip's employer. He knew Sparks, Boots and the others from his prison visits. But how did all this tie up with the drug scene in East London, and Ken's accident?

In the meantime, Philip's request for the band scores gave me the motivation to tackle Ken's private cupboard at last. Steve had given me the key. I had opened it once before and found the band scrap-book, but I couldn't bring myself to delve further. Now it had to be done.

The cupboard seemed to be divided into three sections. The middle related to the horses Ken owned or had an interest in. The lower section had all the clippings and minutes of band meetings, sheet music and so on. It didn't take me long to find the scores Philip wanted.

It was the top section that seemed to hold Ken's personal papers. There was so much. How could anyone collect so much paperwork in such a short lifetime? It was obviously going to take a considerable time to sort through.

I decided to make a start on the band section – that was the easy part. I would get a couple of empty boxes next time I visited the supermarket, put all the band stuff in them and pass them on to Philip. He could sort it all out at his leisure. That would clear at least a third of the cupboard.

I tossed a coin about what section I should start on next, and it came down heads - the top section, all Ken's personal papers. I should have asked Steve to give me a hand with this, but he had a living to make. I decided to sort them into respective groups and give them to Steve. He could decide what to do with them.

I felt I was intruding into Ken's life, but it had to be done, and there was no sense in delaying any longer.

I started rummaging and sorting. It wasn't long before I came across a file which contained a letter from a man called John. I had heard Ken talk about him - he had been at school with Ken and Steve and they had all remained friends. I vaguely remembered Ken saying that John was a good policeman.

I read it through.

"Dear Ken. I'm glad to see you have been leading in some winners lately. I am writing to ask your help. I know how much you despise the people who peddle drugs to youngsters, and I think you may have a couple of contacts that we need some information about. I prefer not to put too much on paper, so can we meet up some time? You can come to my office, or I to yours, or you may prefer dinner one evening, whatever is most convenient for you.

Give me a ring and let me know. Regards, John."

Attached to the letter were several sheets of paper in Ken's handwriting listing initials, dates and various routes from the Continent and from Dover and Harwich. It was all a mystery to me. Time to contact Steve and let him sort it out.

I emailed him, telling him about the file.

Ken rang me a few minutes later.

"It's all beginning to make sense now" he said. "I'd better go and see John. Ken had made no secret of what he thought of the dealers taking advantage of the young people today. He always said we had made our way in life without using of drugs and he couldn't understand why the youngsters needed them."

I knew this was a big point with Ken. He had always appreciated the help he had got in the days, after having to cope with the loss of his parents.

"Ken had done his best to try and stem the flow of drugs, but he didn't feel he was making any impression" Steve went on. "I feel sure this file has something to do with this. I'd better get it to John as quickly as I can. Perhaps Ken was making more headway than we thought."

Mike soon paid Charlie another visit.

"Any news?"

"Well everyone knows Chopper's 'insurance' business has folded, thanks to you."

"What are they up to now?"

"It's as we thought. Sparks says they aren't happy with just acting as distributors, there's not enough in it for them. They want a bigger slice. They want to buy direct. They reckon they know one of the drivers bringing it in. They still think St Paul knows something and they are still threatening him. But it's way out of his league."

"What do they think he knows?"

"He owns a transport company in Suffolk and they think his vehicles are being used. If they are, he'd be the last to know. First sign of trouble he'd spout. He's terrified they'll beat him up."

The next day Mike's phone rang; Charlie. He hadn't wasted much time. "Meet me in the Duke's Head at 6.15" he said. "And don't forget to bring your wallet."

Things looked promising if Charlie was expecting a good drop. Mike had a busy day ahead, as a lot of work was going his way since his success with the market traders. Now he desperately wanted a satisfactory conclusion to the assignment from Steve. It would open the door for him to get more work from legal offices. It was much more prestigious, and he was less likely to have to deal with the likes of the Chopper mob.

Charlie was ready and waiting when Mike arrived.

"Let's get this over pronto Mike, I've got to be at the dogs at seven" said Charlie.

"I'm all ears" Mike responded.

"Do you know of a chap called Speedy? He's a getaway driver. Chopper uses him from time to time. He could compete in any rally – he's the best. Used to be a racing driver and he can still do it. He's also an out-and-out crook, he'd nick his grandmother's tea caddy. But he doesn't do violence. He can't stand the sight of blood. Passes out if you mention a flu jab.

"Can't say I've come across him."

"Well, Speedy's in a right old state at the moment, nerves completely shattered, drinking himself into oblivion. Apparently he said something about not wanting to be mixed up with any killing.

"Killing?" Mike was all ears. This was sounding very interesting indeed.

"They were returning from Portsmouth the day of the Kempton Meeting, they'd been there to pick up a load. Boots was moaning when they got back about the traffic and getting caught up with the racing crowd. Is this beginning to ring any bells?"

"It sure is, just stick with it Charlie. The right answers could earn you a nice little bundle. Give me a ring just as soon as you have anything more about Speedy."

Mike sent his up-to-date report to Steve, telling him he felt they had broken the barriers, and that quite soon all the necessary information would be flooding in. Steve was over the moon.

He hadn't held out much hope when he had first contacted Mike. He had really done it to please Val, but Ken had been such a good mate that anything that could untangle the mystery would be a very good result.

There was a fax from Steve in the machine when I got home. "Val, don't want to raise your hopes too high, but Mick reckons he might be on to something. Will contact you immediately if he comes up with anything else."

John and Steve had arranged to meet for dinner. It was good for both of them. They had both taken the loss of Ken badly, and they had not met up since the funeral.

Steve stowed the file into his briefcase, and hung on to it for dear life while he was on the Tube. After the first few preliminaries and settled with a drink, he handed it to John.

"I respect Ken for keeping this to himself" said John. "We don't spread the word around more than we can help, but I expect you realise by now that Ken had been keeping his eyes and ears open for us for any information that would help in our undercover work.

"Tell me more."

"Briefly, there are far too many drugs getting into the country. We've put in a lot of work over the past year, so we know about most of the vehicles being used. We could pull them up at any time, but we're letting them through – it's a waiting game. We don't want to pick up bits and pieces here and there, we want to smash the whole operation from the source to where it's being stashed. That's the difficult part. We can follow a lorry from the port, but we think the drugs are being transferred to other vehicles en route. Ken's been trying to find out where the swaps take place. I think this is going to be a big help."

"Do you think this had anything to do with Ken's accident?"

"No I don't think so Steve, Ken was very discreet. I doubt if they were aware of his involvement."

Charlie's first port of call after getting the brief from Steve was to go looking for Speedy. He found him in his usual pub and offered him a drink. He eased him away from the bar so that their conversation wouldn't be heard.

"What's the problem Speedy, you don't look too good, got the 'flu?"

The other man looked haggard, as if he was being haunted by something. He scratched his balding head.

"No nothing like that, just a bit of bother."

"No work about for you at the moment?

"There's work, I just don't feel like doing it."

"What sort of work?"

"You know that mob of Chopper's, all brawn and no brains? I'm getting in too deep with them. Makes me nervous."

"I thought that was up your street?"

"Used to be, perhaps. But I'm not a young man any more."

"They making you work too hard?"

"It's the way they do business I'm not keen on. Not my style. That's all."

"So what have they done?"

Speedy went silent for a minute. Charlie took out his wallet and started toying with the leather. Speedy waved it away.

"No money, mate. Look I'll tell you, but it didn't come from me, right?"

"Right."

"They asked me to drive them to Portsmouth in the lorry to pick up a load – I'd never do that again, I've told them, I'm finished with all that. But they made me an offer I couldn't refuse. They also made it clear what would happen if I did refuse."

"You don't need to spell it out, Speedy."

Speedy rolled his eyes. "Well on the way back they got caught up with the race traffic coming out of Kempton, and when we're waiting our turn Boots starts doing his nut. He says he's recognised one of the cars - a BMW. We followed him out into the traffic and Boots is saying, 'that's the bloke Speedy, come on, knock him off the road!' Well of course I'm not going to do any such thing, and Boots is getting even madder. Then Sticks pipes up. 'That's the bastard that tries to stop us getting to the raves and giving the kids a good time' he says. Said he'd know the number plate anywhere, he's seen it so many times.

"Well suddenly they've both got these laser pointers in their hands. Apparently they'd been over to the Continent a couple of weeks previously, and somehow managed to pick them up – they're illegal here now. They had no idea how dangerous they can be. I told them to put them away, but they wouldn't listen. They were hanging out of the side windows. I begged them to be sensible, but I was in the outside lane and couldn't do much to stop them at the time.

"So we pass the BMW and they're pointing these lasers straight at the driver. You could see the red spots dancing around on his face. He was blinking, couldn't work out what had hit him. From what I could see in my mirror he lost control straight away – well, you would, wouldn't you?"

Charlie sat back. This was some piece of news.

"So that's what's bothering you?"

"Yep. It's really got to me, to think that I've worked all my life without any rough stuff at all, and then just when I'm thinking of retiring this should happen. I know I wasn't really responsible for killing that man, but I was the driver."

"Come on Speedy, have another scotch and chaser, make you feel better." He opened the wallet.

"No Charlie, I couldn't. I don't need your money, not for something like this."

A man of honour, thought Charlie. Not so many of those around any more.

Charlie couldn't wait to bring the news to Mike. It was a Wednesday, Charlie's afternoon off from the betting shop, so they met in the lunch hour - not at the Duke's Head as usual but at Charlie's request at the Traveller's Inn, a quiet little pub where they would not be recognised.

"I think I've got to the bottom of the riddle about the car going haywire," said Charlie. He explained what Speedy had told him.

Mike sat back, drumming his fingers on the table.

"You've done very well Charlie, and I really appreciate it. You know I'll be in touch if anything else crops up." He stuffed a large wad of neatly-folded notes into Charlie's top pocket.

The final report from Mike, together with his account, was on Steve's desk when he arrived.

Steve broke the news to me over dinner. In fact he didn't wait for the menus. As soon as I had sat down he handed over a brown envelope containing his final report.

So it had been just a couple of idiots playing with dangerous toys. And the life of the man I had loved had been wasted, for no good reason. I wasn't sure whether I felt relieved at finally knowing what had happened to Ken or even more angry that he had died so unnecessarily.

"What goes round comes around," I said lamely. "I hope they pay for what they did in good time."

"I do feel it was good that we made the effort to prove the accident wasn't down to Ken," said Steve. "Now he will be able to rest in peace."

"Have you heard anything from John?"

"Not yet, but he was very pleased with the file we handed over. He said Ken had been a great help to them with a project they've been working on for the past year to try and stem the flow of drugs entering the country."

It was all over the papers a few days later. According to the Express: "Dawn raids were carried out yesterday on premises and houses in Essex, Kent and East and North London... the drugs seized were the largest haul ever recovered. A number of men and women were taken into custody and are expected to appear in court tomorrow."

So the patient, intricate and very often exhausting work put in over the past year had paid off. It will never stop of course, but it might make it more difficult to get hold of drugs for the time being, and hopefully some young people will be saved from lives of misery.

I wondered about the police raids in East London, hoping particularly that Boots and Sticks, among others, had been rounded up. I even had a little giggle to myself at the thought of the police pouncing on Sticks in bed in his long johns.

CHAPTER FOURTEEN

It was a drizzly, overcast day when the last of the Kray family went to join his mother, father, elder brother Charlie and twin Ronnie at Chingford Mount Cemetery. A suitable day to see off the last member of a family which had put so much fear and unhappiness into other people's lives.

It baffles many police and journalists that so much interest in the Krays still prevails today. Like all the old East End families, their funerals are big events with masses of flowers and lavish headstones. As always, when a well-known person, notorious or otherwise, dies, everyone jumps on the bandwagon to give interviews to the media and write articles about how well they knew the deceased.

A lot of rubbish was said and written about the Krays and how kind they had been to the poor people of Bethnal Green. Of course they only gave away a small part of what they had stolen from other people, and it was mostly to get publicity.

They were fanatical about being photographed with celebrities and would make special journeys to clubs and restaurants in the West End with the sole purpose of standing behind the chair when they spotted a celebrity, photographer at the ready to snap them as though they were best friends.

Why they always wanted a full Church of England service when all their lives they had shown not the slightest sign of Christianity, was always a mystery. Presumably it was because they had to put on a big show right till the end. It's hard to think of anything less appropriate.

When the glass hearse was paraded through the heart of East London to the final resting place at the top of Chingford Mount every street was crowded with onlookers. Every East End hoodlum was there, all dressed in the same black garb.

Apart from those who happened to be guests of Her Majesty at the time, of course. Such as Chopper, Sticks, Boots and the rest of their mob.

* * * * * * * * * *

A few days later Philip called with a letter from the band. It was to ask me to accept the vice-presidency. I was thrilled. I asked him to sit down.

"You know Amanda's been arrested?" he asked me. "She's being held at a police station somewhere in Suffolk."

"Hang on a minute Philip, I don't think I am lipreading you properly - did you say Amanda had been arrested?"

"Yes, yesterday morning - poor old St Paul is taking it very badly."

"But whatever for, what has she done?"

"Amanda was responsible for getting the drugs from the original source into this country. She was financing the operation, working with an old mate of St Paul called Dodgy Duggie. It was Duggie who persuaded Paul to invest in the transport company in the first place, and he ran it for him."

"I can't believe this! Amanda always thought she was so superior to everybody else."

"I know. The police knew she was always at the yard by six am, so they raided her house at four and got her out of bed."

"But why would she get involved with something like this? Surely not for the money. She can't be hard up, and even if she was St Paul would see her right."

"She was the boss. You know she's a woman who has to be in charge. Perhaps the thrill of training winners was wearing a bit thin and she felt the need to be involved with something that was a bit more risky."

"I thought it was St Paul who was being threatened?"

"It was, but they were getting at him to get to her. She's made of sterner stuff than her father and she could hold her own. She was very upset when the horses started dying, but in some strange way it seemed to egg her on to take every greater risks. You know it's been a big worry to me over the past few months, though I didn't know the full extent of it. Amanda kept her dodgy dealings with Duggie well away from my ears. I think it's the end of her husband's hopes of a knighthood."

"Do you think Ken had some idea about Amanda's involvement? You know he took his horses away from her. If he thought had any tie-up with drugs he wouldn't hesitate, he held such strong views about that."

"Poor old Amanda, she won't half notice the difference in Holloway. She won't be able to put on her airs and graces there. They'll soon knock her down a peg or two."

* * * * * * * * * *

I went to early mass the next day. I particularly wanted to have a word with the Holy Mother to thank her for helping me to put the record straight about Ken and restore his good name regarding the accident. John had told Steve how helpful Ken had been about meticulously keeping records of the transport used to distribute the drugs.

I ran out of church to meet the three coaches that were going to make their way to Cheltenham that day. The band had been practising Congratulations, just in case Music Adored should live up to expectations.

The coach for the choir who were to sing with the band were wearing West Ham colours, and of course so was the coach for the boys and girls at the office who had been so loyal and faithful to the Boss's horse.